# LIBBY
### AND THE
## PARISIAN PUZZLE

# LIBBY
## AND THE
# PARISIAN PUZZLE

### JO CLARKE

### ILLUSTRATED BY BECKA MOOR

Firefly

First published in 2022
by Firefly Press
25 Gabalfa Road, Llandaff North, Cardiff, CF14 2JJ
www.fireflypress.co.uk

Text copyright © Jo Clarke 2022
Illustration copyright © Becka Moor 2022

The author and illustrator assert their moral right to
be identified as author and illustrator in accordance
with the Copyright, Designs and Patent Act, 1988.

All rights reserved.
This book is sold subject to the condition that it shall not,
by way of trade or otherwise, be lent, re-sold, hired out or
otherwise circulated without the publisher's prior consent
in any form, binding or cover other than that in which it is
published and without a similar condition including this
condition being imposed on the subsequent purchaser.

All characters in this publication are fictitious
and any resemblance to real persons, living
or dead, is purely coincidental.

A CIP catalogue record of this book is
available from the British Library.

3 5 7 9 8 6 4 2

Print ISBN 9781913102708
ebook ISBN 9781913102715

This book has been published with the support
of the Books Council of Wales.

Typeset and design by Becka Moor

Printed and bound by CPI Group (UK) Ltd, Croydon,
CR0 4YY

MIX
Paper from
responsible sources
FSC
www.fsc.org    FSC® C171272

## JC

For my parents, whose endless support and encouragement made this book possible. Thank you for always believing in me, even when I didn't believe in myself.

## BM

For Jo Clarke, who has been an endless support, not just to me, but to the children's book community as a whole.
We appreciate you.

# MAP of PARIS

1. GARE DU NORD

2. EIFFEL TOWER

3. SCHOOL

4. BATEUX MOUCHES

5. LOUVRE

6. PLACE DU TERTE

7. CAFE

8. LIBRARY

9. POMPIDOU CENTRE

10. ARC DE TRIOMPHE

11. OPERA GARNIER

12. PATISSERIE

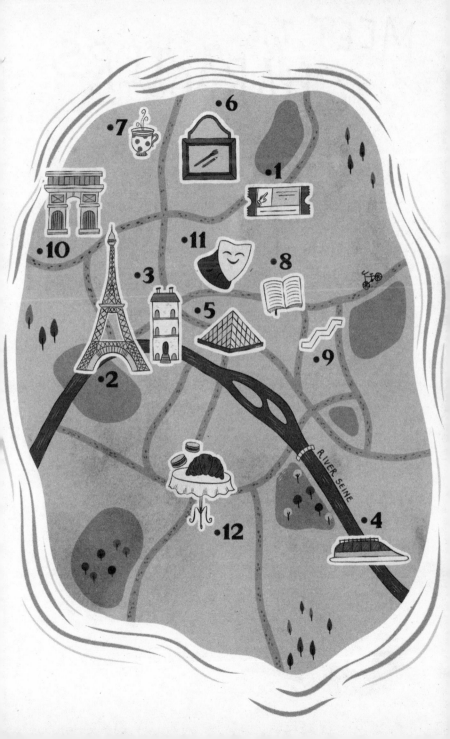

# MEET THE CHARACTERS

LIBBY

CONNIE

AUNT AGATHA

MISS WALL

MISS BROWNE

NOAH

SEBASTIAN

JOCELYN

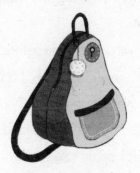

# Chapter 1
## All Aboard

Libby couldn't believe her luck. The train was half empty and she'd managed to bag a whole table to herself. She shoved her case into the space behind her seat. Her mum waved frantically at the window. Checking no one was watching, Libby kneeled on her seat, opened the window and shouted, 'Are you really sure I can't come to Ecuador with you?'

'I've told you, Libby, it's too difficult this time. You'll be fine with Aunt Agatha.'

Her mum looked loaded down with her huge

rucksack and was wearing her sunglasses despite the dull weather.

'But you've always taken me before.' Libby thought about all the different places they'd travelled together. They'd sailed down rivers in rickety old boats, flown in seaplanes, sled across frozen lands.

'I know and if I could take you with me, I would. I'll miss you, Libby … but you'll be having far too much fun in Paris to miss me.' Her mum smiled just a little too brightly.

Libby sighed. If only her dad was still here, maybe she wouldn't have to go away. Although she was actually looking forward to Paris, it was one of her absolute favourite places – but she knew it wouldn't be the same without Mum.

When her mum had first suggested the school, Libby was horrified. She'd never been to school before; they'd never stayed in one place long enough. But at the same time, she had always wondered what it would be like to go, and she was fascinated by the idea of the school her aunt ran. She really hoped it wasn't like she imagined it, though – children all lined up in rows wearing stiff uniforms. That would be awful!

Aunt Agatha was no ordinary head teacher. She ran Mousedale's Travelling School. Each term they moved to a different place: one term they might be sleeping in a treehouse on a remote island; another in an apartment in New York overlooking Central Park! She was joining the school for a term in Paris.

'Mum, did you pack my camera?'

Libby's mum took pictures for travel magazines and Libby had inherited her talent and love for photography.

'It's in your rucksack with Bonnie.'

Libby felt her neck redden. 'Mum!' As much as she loved her tatty bunny, Bonnie, she didn't want the whole world knowing she still took her everywhere.

Mum laughed. 'Call me if you have any problems.'

Libby nodded. Her mum had given her an old mobile. All she could do on it was call and text, but Libby had never had a phone before, so it was still a treat.

Her mum looked at her watch.

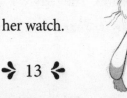

'I really need to go if I'm going to catch my flight.'

She was smiling but Libby could tell she was reluctant to leave her. Her mum always twisted her hair when she was stressed.

'Have a fabulous time, Libby. And try not to get in any trouble. Remember, not everything is a mystery waiting for you to solve it.'

Her mum wiped away a tear. Libby would normally be embarrassed, but her own stomach felt twisty – this was the first time in her life they'd be apart for longer than a single night. Butterflies danced inside her the more she thought about it, but she didn't want to upset her mum.

'I promise,' she said.

But, if a mystery just happened to find her, well, she couldn't help that…

Her mum rushed off, with a last worried look over her shoulder. Libby sat back and took a deep breath. She was alone. It was really happening.

A woman entered her carriage. Libby was glad of the distraction. The lady was clinging to a battered red suitcase. A guard came down the aisle, saw her struggling with her case and tried to help her. There were raised voices. Libby couldn't quite make out what was being said, but it was clear the lady didn't want to let go of it. The guard gave up, turned swiftly on his heel and headed to Libby.

He leaned over and smiled. 'Ticket?'

Libby handed it to him. The railway company's special hologram sparkled in the sunlight. Her mum had bought her a special ticket so the guards would look out for her. The guard said, in a French accent, 'Let me know if you need anything, during the journey or when we arrive.'

Libby didn't want to be treated like a baby. 'My aunt is meeting me at the station in Paris.'

'Well, that is good.' He smiled and off he went to the next carriage.

The woman with the red case had found a seat now. She kept looking behind her, as if she was expecting someone else. She fiddled with the buttons on her cardigan and Libby couldn't help noticing a large green ring on her finger.

Libby looked out of the window, hoping for one

last glimpse of her mum, even though she knew she was long gone. A tall lady came hurtling down the platform, her black-and-white coat flying behind her like a cape. She was waving, trying to get the attention of the guard, who was about to blow his whistle. Just as the doors were closing, she leaped on to the train, holding on to her blue hat.

Libby felt the pull of the train and the screech of the brakes releasing. They were off.

Before long, they were whizzing along at an amazing speed. Libby snuggled into her thick fleece and got comfy. The tall lady who had just managed to get on the train in time peered into the carriage. Libby wondered if she was looking for an empty seat. She must have changed her mind, because she disappeared in the other direction. Libby glimpsed a bright peacock feather swish at the back of her hat as she turned.

Libby checked her watch. It was still *ages* till they arrived in Paris. With no one to stop her, she could start on her lunch, even if it wasn't strictly lunchtime. She moved her watch forward an hour ready for her

arrival in Paris – now she could eat! Her lunch box was crammed with slices of cheese and breadsticks and nestling at the bottom was a slab of chocolate cake. She scooped up a big blob of hummus, then the train rocked, making her drop a splodge on her dungarees. She wiped at it – she didn't want to meet everyone at the school looking a mess.

Wiping the last crumb of cake off her lips, she looked around again. The lady was still holding her suitcase tightly and she seemed very stressed. Maybe she got travel sick – or maybe she had a secret to hide. The lady glanced up and spotted Libby. Embarrassed to be caught staring, Libby quickly turned to look at a man at the table opposite. He was reading a newspaper. She could just make out an article about a missing ring before he turned the page.

Libby remembered her mum's warning about poking her nose into things. So she rummaged around in her rucksack and found her new *Isobel Investigates* book. Libby had been so busy packing what she really needed – her entire collection of animal-rubber-topped pencils; puzzle books; a secret stash of jellybeans – that she hadn't had the chance to read it yet. Isobel was her favourite sleuth, who managed to solve even the most tricky of cases.

Libby had just got to a part where Isobel found a coded letter when a shadow fell across her page. She looked up. The window had gone dark. They were finally entering the Channel Tunnel. She was on the way to Paris all by herself.

# Chapter 2
## Trouble in Paris

'Ladies and gentlemen. *Mesdames et messieurs.*
We will shortly be arriving in Paris,' said the
announcement.

Libby had been so engrossed in her book, she
hadn't noticed the train pulling into the Gare du
Nord. She was *absolutely* starving and her tummy
rumbled. Her mum would say that would teach her
for having her lunch so early.

Everyone in the carriage started to head
to the doors and the aisles were quickly
jammed with people. A small girl
with pigtails was nearly squashed

by the large bag of the man behind her. Libby decided she'd wait.

She looked out at the crowded platform and a fizz of excitement bubbled inside her. She couldn't believe she was finally in Paris. *What an adventure I'm going to have*, she thought.

When she finally walked down the aisle, she noticed that the lady with the suitcase was fast asleep. Now Libby was closer, she could see the green ring clearly. It looked like a very large emerald but it was so big it couldn't possibly be real.

Libby felt bad – what if this woman ended up going all the way back to London? She looked round. Surely someone would wake her? But everyone else was in too much of a hurry to notice.

She leaned over and tapped her gently on the shoulder. 'Sorry to disturb you. We've just arrived in Paris,' Libby whispered, not wishing to startle her.

The lady jumped awake and hugged her case to her chest. She smiled at Libby and then stared closely at her, as if she recognised her. 'Thank you. I can't believe I fell asleep!'

Libby smiled then made her way down the carriage to the exit.

She got off the train, set down her bag and looked around. She could see guards on the platform, helping people with their luggage, but there was no sign of her Aunt Agatha. It was strange. She was never late.

She spotted the tall lady with the black-and-white coat. Unlike everyone else, she seemed in no rush to leave the station. Looking closely, Libby could see she was searching up and down, as if waiting for someone else to get off the train. But nobody joined her. Libby steered her suitcase through the bustling crowds to the grand exit, trying not to bang into people. Maybe her Aunt Agatha was waiting outside. She looked up at the curved glass roof, but there was no sun shining through. It looked like a really miserable day.

As she reached the entrance, her heart sank. The rain was absolutely hammering down, creating huge puddles on the pavement. And there was no sign of her aunt. She was sure her mum had said Aunt Agatha was meeting her at the station. But she hadn't really been listening – she'd been too busy packing her bags. What if she'd got it completely wrong? Paris didn't feel like an adventure anymore. Tears pricked at her eyes.

'Are you okay? You look a bit lost,' came a voice from behind her.

Libby turned around and saw the lady who'd been asleep. She was still carrying her red suitcase, but Libby noticed she was no longer wearing her ring. She hoped she hadn't lost it.

'I'm fine, thank you.' She tried not to make eye contact. She didn't want anyone to see her tears. She wasn't sure how much longer she could hold them in.

'Is there someone you can call?' The woman stepped towards Libby and smiled. 'Or maybe I can help? It's the least I can do after you woke me up.'

Libby knew her mum wouldn't want her to talk to a stranger. Why did the lady keep asking her questions? She wished her aunt would hurry up! Where could she be?

'I'm waiting for my Aunt Agatha,' said Libby, trying to sound confident. 'She's picking me up. I'm starting at her school on Monday.'

'Agatha? Your aunt doesn't happen to be Agatha Mousedale?'

'Yes,' said Libby, surprised.

'I'm Louisa Browne. I work at your aunt's school!' She had a lovely smile. 'Your aunt told me you might be on the train. I'm surprised she's not here.'

'So she definitely knew I was coming today?'

Libby had no idea *what* to do. Maybe she could phone Mum. She checked her watch and sighed. Her mum would be on the plane by now.

*Come on, Libby, think,* she told herself. Scrolling through her mum's contacts list on her phone, she spotted her aunt's name and smiled.

'It's fine, I'll call her,' she said.

Libby felt anything but fine. Her palms were sweaty and she nearly dropped her phone when it started to beep. 'Oh, it's making a weird noise!' Today was turning out to be a disaster!

'Probably means you don't have a signal. I'll ring

her and find out where she is.' Miss Browne searched through her handbag and took out her own phone.

A piece of paper fell out of her bag at the same time, but she didn't notice. Libby reached down to pick it up. It looked as if it had been torn out of a newspaper.

'Miss Browne, you've dropped this,' she said. But the teacher was too busy talking to hear.

Libby sighed. Was she going to have to get across Paris by herself? She got out her map of the métro and popped Miss Browne's piece of paper into her pocket so she didn't lose it. Staring at the map didn't help. It was so confusing, with so many different lines and stops. She even tried turning it upside down to see if that helped.

'I have your aunt for you.' Miss Browne smiled.

'Aunt Agatha?' said Libby. She almost cried in relief to hear her voice. 'Are you nearly here?'

'I'm so sorry, Libby. The road is blocked and I couldn't get a taxi.'

After a frantic apology from her aunt, it was agreed that Libby would go with Miss Browne to the school. Libby sighed – it wasn't the best start to her adventure!

They headed to the taxi rank. A long queue of people were trying to shelter from the rain. Libby glimpsed a swish of black-and-white pass them. It looked like the other lady from the train, although she couldn't be sure as she was hidden under a large umbrella.

Libby pulled up her hood, but the rain was so fierce, drops landed on her nose. She put her hands in her pocket and found the piece of newspaper Miss Browne had dropped.

'I think this is yours.' She held it out to Miss Browne.

'What? How did you get hold of that?' Miss Browne snatched it. She looked panicked.

Libby stepped back. 'You dropped it … er … back in the station,' she stuttered.

'Sorry, I didn't mean to snap. It's my own fault. I should be more careful. It's very sentimental to me.' Miss Browne hastily smiled and put her arm round Libby. 'When we get to school, how about you and me share this box of macarons?'

'Ooh, macarons, my favourite.' Libby had tried macarons last time she was in Paris. The patisseries were full of these rainbow-coloured sweet treats and she grinned as she remembered the crunch as she bit into them and how they melted on her tongue.

But she wondered what was on that piece of paper? Strange that Miss Browne was so agitated when she handed it back. She wished she'd had a sneak peek when she'd had the chance.

'*Cette adresse, s'il vous plaît,*' said Miss Browne, handing a piece of paper to the driver when it was their turn, and the taxi sped them away. Libby stared out of the window. The school was somewhere near the Eiffel Tower. She had only been eight when she was last in Paris, but she still remembered how magical the tower was, especially at night when its lights burst out of the darkness, scattering rays of colour across the city.

The city was very busy and the taxi lurched in and out of the traffic, stopping abruptly then speeding off again. They crossed the river to the Left Bank. Libby tried to visualise the map of Paris in her head.

Her mum had helped her learn it before she came. Their driver kept beeping his horn and raising his fist at the cars in front. She realised that she was so lost in her own thoughts, she hadn't said a word to Miss Browne.

'Have you been to Paris before?' she asked.

'No, I don't know anyone in Paris … well, except for your aunt. Oh, and now you, of course. This is my first term at the school.'

'It's my first term too,' said Libby. 'I think we're going to New York next.'

Miss Browne's eyes lit up. 'Yes, I'm really looking forward to that.'

'Me too,' said Libby. 'I'm going to go to one of those diners where the waiters are on roller skates and eat a huge, ice-cream sundae, just like in the films.'

Miss Browne smiled. 'That sounds like an excellent plan.'

The taxi swerved sharply round the corner, throwing Libby and Miss Browne forward. Miss Browne gasped and clutched her suitcase. *'Faites attention!'* she shouted at the driver. He shrugged and muttered something under his breath.

'You must have something special in there,' said Libby, surprised at Miss Browne's reaction. 'I'm the same with my rucksack; it's stuffed with all my favourite things.'

Miss Browne frowned.

The taxi veered off down a busy street. Despite the rain, there were lots of people sitting outside restaurants, huddled under heaters. Suddenly the taxi slammed to a halt, throwing them forward.

'Looks like we're here,' Miss Browne said. 'Let's get inside, it's freezing.'

Libby took a deep breath and looked out at the tall building in front of them. Although it was getting dark, she could make out vines climbing up the walls and she could see balconies on the top floors. Looking around, she thought she could spot the Eiffel Tower twinkling in the distance, but the sky was so thick with clouds she couldn't be sure.

'Libby!' shouted a voice. Libby turned. At the top of the steps stood her aunt, her hair tied up in a loose bun with pens sticking out at odd angles, her bright yellow dress a warm contrast to the gloomy day.

'Aunt Agatha!' yelled Libby. Rushing up the steps, she threw herself into her aunt's arms and squeezed her tightly.

'I'm so sorry I wasn't there to meet you, Libby,' said her aunt. 'How's your mum? What was the journey like? Tell me everything!'

Over her aunt's shoulder, Libby couldn't help but notice how Miss Browne was staring into the distance. It seemed as if she was looking for someone. *How strange*, thought Libby. *She said she didn't know anyone here.*

# CHAPTER 3
## A New Friend

Libby rubbed her eyes sleepily. She gazed at the light streaming through the unfamiliar, thin curtains, frowned and then remembered. She was in Paris! She jumped out of bed, ran to the window and pushed it open.

'*Bonjour*, Paris!' she shouted, leaning out.

A very glamorous woman walking her dachshund in the street looked up and the dog yapped in reply. Libby giggled and ducked back inside.

The sun was shining and Paris looked so pretty, such a difference from the day before. All along the cobbled street, she could see stalls and shops filled with freshly baked bread, large domes of cheese and piles of pastries, and the cafés were bustling with people chatting and drinking coffee. There were parents rushing around holding drinks and long, thin loaves of bread, while clutching small children's hands.

She wondered what her mum was doing now and whether she felt as if a part of her was missing too.

But the sight of all the yummy food made her stomach rumble. It was definitely time for breakfast. Slipping her fluffy slippers onto her feet, she wrapped her dressing gown around herself and bounded down the stairs.

Aunt Agatha sat by the window, reading a newspaper. She was the only person in the dining room.

'At last, there you are. It's almost nine o'clock,' she said, looking over her glasses. She poured Libby a large cup of hot chocolate. 'Help yourself to breakfast.'

'Morning, Aunt Agatha,' said Libby, popping a kiss on her aunt's cheek.

Her eyes widened at the piles of delicious-looking pastries. Grabbing two, she started tucking into them, scattering flakes of croissant everywhere.

'I'm *so* tired.' Libby let out a huge yawn.

'Libby, try not to talk with your mouth full, you're getting crumbs all over the table,' laughed her aunt. 'Mrs Roux will tell me off if we leave the dining room in a mess.'

'Sorry, Aunt Agatha.' Libby tried her best to nibble delicately. She felt like a hamster and had to stifle giggles.

'Libby, while I remember, do call me Aunt Agatha when it's the two of us. But when the others arrive, remember it's Miss Mousedale. I don't want to be accused of having favourites.' She winked.

'I'll try.' Libby smiled. 'It'll be a bit strange, though.' She looked around the room. 'Has Miss Browne slept in as well?'

'No, unlike you, young lady, she was up first thing,' her aunt teased. 'Apparently she had an errand to run.'

'She seems nice. Last night she popped in to check on me before bedtime.' Libby decided not to mention the macarons. She didn't think her aunt would approve of late-night feasts.

'I'm glad you're settling in already. You must be missing your mum.'

'A bit.' She hoped she might have had a message to say her mum had arrived, but so far she'd heard nothing.

Libby wondered why Miss Browne had got up so early on a Sunday, especially when there was hot chocolate and pastries on offer. *All the more for me,* she thought, ripping open another croissant, smothering it with jam and topping up her drink. Maybe being away from home wasn't so bad after all.

Her aunt checked her watch. 'Time to get dressed, Libby. The other students will start arriving from ten.'

Libby headed upstairs. The idea of all the other children arriving unsettled her. Spotting her rucksack on the floor, she tipped everything out. There was so much stuff, she couldn't believe she'd managed to cram it all in. At the top of the pile was a small photo frame – a picture of her with her mum.

*Why couldn't you take me this time?* Libby thought.

She still didn't understand her mum saying she couldn't go with her to Ecuador. They'd travelled to many remote places before.

Her bunny Bonnie was peeping out from under her duvet. She quickly hid her under the pillow, not wanting anyone to make fun of her for still having a cuddly toy. She placed the photo frame on the bedside table and started stuffing everything else back in her rucksack.

A loud creak startled her. Standing at the door was a girl who looked about the same age as Libby, although she was much taller. Her hair was curly and wild, at odds with her smart, checked trousers and green coat. She made Libby feel scruffy. The girl was carrying an old red case, which looked as stuffed as Libby's had been.

Libby waited, but the girl stared at her shoes, refusing to make eye contact. So she leaped up. 'Hi, I'm Libby. I'm from London. Where are you from?'

'Errm…' Her voice was so low Libby could barely hear her.

'Actually, let me see if I can figure it out.' Libby paced

up and down the room. 'I'm guessing that you've come a long way. From … er … Scotland.'

The girl's eyes widened.

'And your name is… Don't tell me…' Libby paused. 'It's Connie,' she said, a huge grin spreading across her face.

'What? How did you guess?' asked Connie.

'And you have a large dog, maybe two. Golden retriever?'

Connie sat down on the bed and stared at her. 'Are you some kind of magician?'

'More of a detective,' Libby laughed. 'Your case has the Scottish flag on it, and your name is on your luggage label. Oh, and as for the dogs, I took a wild guess when I spotted the hairs on your trousers.'

'I really thought you were some kind of mind-reader.' Connie giggled and lay back on the bed. 'Oh, it's been a long day.'

'Are you new as well?' Before Connie had a chance to reply, Libby carried on. 'I've always travelled with my mum till now, but she says "it's too difficult" to take me this time.'

'Nothing that exciting. My mum thinks my brother is a bad influence on me,' said Connie. 'Apparently walking through muddy fields and climbing trees is not "ladylike behaviour".'

'Who wants to be ladylike?' laughed Libby.

'Exactly!' said Connie. 'My mum has known Miss Mousedale since school and she thought this might be a more suitable place for me.'

'Ha!' Libby grinned. 'Good job your mum hasn't met me. I'm definitely not a *suitable* influence.'

'Excellent,' said Connie. 'I was hoping you'd say that.'

Connie began unpacking her suitcase. Libby watched her carefully putting her clothes into her drawers and hoped she didn't notice Libby's pile of clothes still on the floor. She nudged them under her bed with her foot.

'Is this your first time in Paris?'

'Yes,' said Connie. 'I bet it's way more exciting than home. I live in the middle of nowhere.'

'I'm sure it's not that bad?' said Libby.

'Honestly, it's worse! Our nearest neighbours are

three miles away and it's an hour's drive to any shop!'

'Well, Paris will definitely be different then! I think we're going on the Bateaux Mouches this morning, sailing along the Seine,' said Libby. 'You'll be able to see the whole of Paris.' She looked out of the open window. Despite the sun, a cold blast of air made her shiver. 'It's freezing.'

'I'm used to the cold. It's practically arctic where I live,' said Connie. 'I really hope we get to see the Eiffel Tower.'

Libby sat down on the bed next to her. 'We definitely will. Let's go before Aunt … I mean, Miss Mousedale goes without us.'

Connie stared at her. 'You're not going out like that?'

Libby looked down. In all the excitement, she had forgotten she was still wearing her pyjamas. Quickly, she changed into her dungarees and a stripy top.

'Girls, are you ready? We're waiting for you,' boomed a voice from the bottom of the stairs.

'Coming, Miss Mousedale,' they both said.

Libby looked at Connie. 'Jinx,' she said, and they ran down the stairs.

# CHAPTER 4
## Bateaux Mouches

Libby looked round the dining room. The tables were filled with students chatting away. Most of them looked *way* older than her and Connie. She could see her aunt was trying to get everyone's attention.

'Quiet,' said Miss Mousedale, raising her voice over the noise. The volume gradually faded to a low murmur. 'Welcome back, everyone. I hope you've all had a lovely summer.' She smiled. 'I can hear that lots of you are catching up, if the noise is anything to go by.'

A few giggles scattered across the room. Everyone seemed to like her aunt.

'We're pleased to welcome some new pupils this year. Libby, Connie, Sebastian and Noah are joining us, alongside our new teacher, Miss Browne. I want you to make them all welcome.' She paused and smiled at Libby and Connie. 'Let's show them how Mousedale's Travelling School embraces every new country we visit, in our own unique way of exploring, learning and creating. I'm sure we'll fill our journals with lots of different experiences during our term in Paris.'

Libby looked round the room at all the smiling faces and began to relax. She couldn't wait to meet everyone. Glancing over, she could see that Connie's neck was all blotchy. Clearly she didn't feel comfortable with all the attention.

Strangely, there was no sign of Miss Browne. Surely she should be here to meet the students?

Two boys sat in the corner. One smiled at her. The other seemed to be completely distracted, not listening to her aunt. They had heads of dark, tight curls and were clearly identical twins. *I wonder if that's Sebastian and Noah?* Libby thought.

'We'll be leaving in five minutes to start exploring the city and I don't think there's a better way to see Paris than a trip down the Seine. Make sure you wrap up, it's chilly outside. We're not in Madrid anymore,' said Mrs Mousedale, laughing at her own joke. 'And stay together – Miss Browne can't join us, as she's not feeling well, so I need to know where you all are.'

'Let's say hi,' said Libby, grabbing Connie's hand and dragging her over to the boys in the corner. They looked to be the same age, but when they stood up, they both towered over Libby.

One of them held out his hand. 'I'm Sebastian and this is my twin brother Noah … and yes, we are identical, before you ask.'

Libby looked at Connie, puzzled. It was a bit weird to shake hands but she didn't want to offend Sebastian on the first day.

'Oww!' Libby felt a sharp pain in her hand as their hands touched, like being stung by a bee. She shrieked and jumped back.

'Noah! I can't believe you did that!' The other boy elbowed his brother. 'Ignore him, he's always playing pranks. And *I'm* Seb, *he's* Noah. He thinks he's hilarious.'

Noah grinned and opened his hand to reveal a small black box. 'Sorry, didn't mean to hurt you. It only gives a *small* shock,' he said, innocently.

*What an idiot*, thought Libby. But she smiled broadly – she wasn't going to give him the satisfaction of knowing he'd hurt her. 'Very funny!'

She turned and rolled her eyes at Connie. Behind them, she could hear Seb telling his brother off.

'C'mon, Libby,' said Connie. 'Let's go or they'll leave without us!'

\*\*\*

It was freezing on the top deck of the bateaux-mouche, but Libby convinced Connie that the views were worth it. Sebastian and Noah had also braved the cold; she could see them at the far end of the deck. Everyone else was down below, keeping warm.

'My hands are going blue,' moaned Connie, rubbing them together. 'I didn't think it was possible for anywhere to be colder than home.'

'But look at everything we can see up here!' said
Libby, turning Connie around.

To their right, they had a wonderful view of the
Eiffel Tower in the distance. It towered above the
buildings and almost seemed to touch the clouds.

'Wow,' said Connie. 'It's huge.'

'Wait till the way back, then you'll see it close up.' Libby took her camera out of her bag. 'I'd better take some photos. I promised I'd send some to my mum.'

She happily snapped shots as they went under each of the bridges. Some were ordinary, but she was drawn to a really beautiful bridge with ornate gold figures. Scrolling back as the boat moved on, to check she had the shots she'd wanted, Libby spotted someone.

'Connie. That's Miss Browne.' She pointed at her screen. Libby zoomed in to take a closer look.

Their teacher was talking to an older man on the top of the bridge. He looked annoyed. There was nothing distinctive about him except he was wearing a bow tie, which Libby thought was quite unusual.

'I thought she was staying behind with a migraine?' said Connie.

'I know that,' said Libby. 'But I'm sure it's her. And they look as if they're arguing.'

'How can you tell that from a photo?' asked Connie. 'It's not even that clear.'

'Look how he's waving his arms at her,' said Libby. 'Something odd is going on!'

'Ask her later, if you're so sure it's her,' teased Connie.

Libby laughed. 'You want me to say, "Er, Miss Browne, why did you lie and say you were at home sick?"'

'Now can you hear how silly you sound?' said Connie. 'It must be someone who looks like her.'

'That must be it.' Libby still wasn't convinced, though.

She pulled her scarf closer around her neck. She should have worn her thicker coat; she was bitterly cold. Suddenly, she spotted the Louvre coming into view. 'Look, Connie.'

Connie's eyes lit up. 'I've been dying to go there. I really want to see the *Mona Lisa*.'

'I'm sure you will. Shall we go downstairs? I'm freezing.'

'Definitely,' agreed Connie. 'I thought you'd never ask.'

***

Back at school, the girls went to defrost in front of the fire. There were only a few other students in the dining room, so it wasn't as noisy as it had been that morning. Connie definitely seemed more relaxed. Travelling around so much, Libby had never had the chance to make proper friends, so she was really happy to be sharing a room with Connie. The two girls warmed their hands on their mugs of hot chocolate and squished into the window seat. Libby wanted to talk to Connie, without anyone else overhearing.

'I looked at the photo again and I'm positive it was Miss Browne,' Libby whispered.

'But why would she lie?' asked Connie.

Libby shrugged her shoulders. 'Maybe she has something to hide.'

The door opened and Miss Browne walked in. Libby flushed. She hoped the teacher hadn't overheard what she'd said. But she couldn't miss this chance. What if this was an actual, real-life mystery waiting to be solved?

'Look here's Miss Browne now,' said Libby, a little too loudly.

Miss Browne looked up. 'Hi, Libby,' she smiled. 'And you must be … Connie?'

'Yes,' said Connie. 'Are you feeling better?'

'Better?' she asked. Then she blushed slightly. 'Much better, thank you. My migraine has almost gone.' She moved across the room away from them.

Libby raised her eyebrows at Connie.

'What?' Connie gave Libby a puzzled look.

'I told you something was up,' Libby mouthed.

Connie just shrugged her shoulders. She sipped her hot chocolate. 'That's better – I can almost feel my toes again.'

'You girls must be frozen,' said Miss Browne, staring out of the window.

Libby nudged Connie. 'She'd only know that if she'd been outside. It looks really sunny.'

Connie glared back. She said loudly, 'It was brilliant. Shame you missed it.'

'There'll be plenty of time for me to explore,' said Miss Browne.

Miss Mousedale came in. She smiled at the girls and then spotted Miss Browne perched on the edge of a chair. 'Louisa, you're up! I hope you're feeling better.' She handed her an envelope.

'A letter for me? But there's no address on it.' Miss

Browne looked confused. 'Nobody knows I'm here!'

'It was delivered by hand. The concierge just brought it up,' said Miss Mousedale.

'Who would do that?' she snapped.

Libby was watching carefully. Why was Miss Browne so agitated about a letter?

'More hot chocolate, Connie?' she asked and walked over to the table to get a closer look.

Miss Browne's hands trembled as she opened the envelope. Inside there was another envelope, which Libby thought was very strange. The teacher's face turned blotchy, and panic flashed in her eyes. Libby recognised that reaction from the train station.

Miss Browne stuffed the letter in her pocket without even reading it. 'I think my migraine is back,' she said, her eyes filling with tears. 'I need to lie down.'

She left the room, slamming the door. Connie looked at Libby. 'I wonder what was in the letter?'

'I don't know; she didn't even read it,' said Libby. 'But, something isn't quite right and I'm going to find out! Who knows? Maybe she's in trouble and needs our help.'

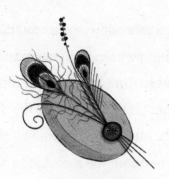

# CHAPTER 5
## Lost in the Louvre

The first few weeks flew by and Libby was so busy she didn't have the chance to feel homesick. Any time a tiny bit of sadness crept over her, she could always count on Connie to cheer her up.

When she'd found out she was going to a travelling school, she hadn't realised there would be *so* much time spent studying. Libby found it really tricky to sit still at her desk. Her feet got all fidgety and she was forever being told off for gazing out of the window. On her travels with her mum, the lessons had been more practical. She had not learned much algebra, but she could figure her way round a train timetable and translate a menu in a restaurant. Luckily, she always sat next to Connie, who made brilliant notes and nudged her if she was getting too distracted.

Most nights Miss Browne would pop into their room before bedtime for a chat. She would often bring them treats and make them laugh with her terrible jokes, so Libby couldn't help but like her. She started to forget about the day Miss Browne had behaved so strangely.

One night, Libby and Connie were playing an old board game that Connie had brought from home. You had to find out who was the murderer. Libby always won.

There was a knock and Miss Browne popped her head round the door. 'Girls, I've brought you some macarons from the patisserie we passed earlier. I couldn't resist.'

Libby looked at the different flavours, trying to decide which one to try first. She reached for a yellow one and popped the whole thing in her mouth, enjoying the tangy, sweet, lemon taste. She passed them to Connie, who chose the pink one, and Miss Browne took the purple one – they all had their favourites. Miss Browne sat on the edge of Libby's bed. Her hair was twisted up in knots, which made her look even younger than normal. She could almost be mistaken for a sixth former in her checked pyjamas and fluffy dressing gown.

'Miss Browne, please play,' begged Connie. 'Otherwise Libby will win again.'

Libby threw a cushion at Connie. 'Oi, that's not fair. I can't help being the best detective.'

Connie threw the cushion back. 'I can't help being the best detective,' she mimicked.

'Okay, how can I refuse?' laughed Miss Browne.

Just as it looked as though Libby might win again, Miss Mousedale shouted from downstairs, 'Lights out in five minutes.'

'You heard Miss Mousedale. Bedtime, girls,' said Miss Browne.

'Not fair,' moaned Libby, throwing the dice across the board.

'Sorry, Libby. We've a busy day tomorrow, so brush your teeth and get ready for bed.'

'I can't believe we're finally going to the Louvre,' said Connie, excitedly.

'Oh, I *forgot* that was tomorrow,' said Miss Browne. Libby noticed a flash of annoyance in her eyes as she slammed the lid on the box. 'Enough complaining. It's time for bed!'

'What's up with her?' asked Connie, after Miss Browne left the room.

Libby shook her head. 'Why be so grumpy about an art gallery?'

'She's probably worried about what Noah will get up to this time,' laughed Connie.

'Remember when were at the Musée d'Orsay and he left his rucksack by the statues!' Libby rolled her eyes.

'The security guard was furious. Good job we realised before they had to evacuate the museum,' Connie agreed.

\*\*\*

Streams of tourists wound round the glass pyramids and Libby felt as if they'd been waiting in the queue for *hours*! Connie and Sebastian were chattering away non-stop.

Sebastian was quizzing Connie, 'What do you want to see?'

'Definitely the *Mona Lisa*,' said Connie. 'I can't wait to sketch it!'

Restless and looking around, Libby noticed Miss Browne kept checking her watch. Perhaps she was bored too. The queue seemed to have come to a complete stop.

Noah was fooling around, jumping in and out of the line.

'Noah, will you behave!' Miss Browne snapped. 'Just keep still for one minute!'

'I wasn't…' Noah complained, but Miss Browne ignored him.

'This is your last chance, Noah,' she warned.

Libby thought Noah was annoying, but she still felt Miss Browne was being really hard on him. A gust of wind sent shivers down her back. She pulled down her hat so it almost touched her nose and tucked her hands into her sleeves.

'We'll be too cold to draw anything by the time we get in,' she moaned.

Connie laughed. 'Well, if our sketches are awful, it's the perfect excuse.'

When they finally managed to get inside the Louvre, Libby watched Connie look round in wonder.

Miss Browne called them all together. 'Remember, stay in your pairs. I don't want anyone getting lost,' she said. 'Now, you can explore anywhere but you must meet me back here at one for lunch.'

Everyone disappeared in different directions, glad to be free of their teacher. Libby wanted to ask Miss Browne the quickest way to the *Mona Lisa*, but their teacher dashed away into the crowd. *She seems in a hurry,* thought Libby. Before she could wonder why, she was distracted by Connie tugging her coat.

'Libby, the *Mona Lisa*.' Connie pointed to her map.

They forced their way through the crowds up the spiral stairs to the gallery, squeezing past a large group of schoolchildren having their photo taken. You could barely move for people eager for a glimpse of the famous painting.

Connie pushed her way to the front, dragging Libby behind her. 'Oh, it's quite small,' said Connie, clearly disappointed. She stared at the painting locked away behind glass.

'Yes, it's *really* small,' said Libby. She snapped a picture, her reflection bouncing off the glass. 'Still, we better do some drawing. Miss Browne is in a foul mood and we don't want to get told off.'

Finding a place to sit, they both sketched the painting. Libby was trying to mimic Mona Lisa's smile, but her version looked lopsided, more like a Picasso.

'I give up,' moaned Libby. 'I'm rubbish at drawing.' She peered over at Connie's sketchpad. 'That's brilliant!'

Connie blushed. 'I'd love to come back to Paris after school to paint. It's all I've ever wanted to do. But my dad doesn't think being an artist is a proper job.'

'Oh, now I see,' said Libby. 'That's why you said you were so desperate to come here. I didn't realise.

I'm definitely losing my detecting ability!'

Libby, bored of sketching, started people watching. It was her favourite thing to do. After a few minutes of nothing at all mysterious, she spotted Miss Browne talking to someone. A peacock feather caught her eye – a peacock feather on the hat of the woman Miss Browne was talking to. She could see Miss Browne shaking her head furiously and she could hear raised voices. Were they arguing?

Libby wondered if she could get nearer without being noticed. She stood up and moved closer, pretending to look at the *Mona Lisa* again.

'I'm not who you think I am!' insisted Miss Browne.

Libby started. *Who did the woman think Miss Browne was*? Before she could get any closer, the other woman stormed off. Miss Browne turned and when she made eye contact with Libby, her face looked like thunder.

Just then a group of tourists walked between them and by the time they'd passed Miss Browne had disappeared.

'Libby, are you listening to me?' asked Connie as she walked back.

'Sorry… I've just seen Miss Browne arguing with a woman. She looked furious when she realised I'd seen her.'

'What, again?'

'What do you mean?' said Libby.

'You said she was arguing with that man on the bridge. It's a bit of a coincidence, Libby, that you always seem to see her doing something mysterious.'

'Maybe I'm just observant,' said Libby. 'Isobel says a good detective should always be on the lookout for clues.'

'Isobel? Are you talking about those books again?

No wonder you always think everything is suspicious.'

Libby blushed. To be fair, in the short time they had known each other, she had been convinced there was a mystery to solve when her notebook had gone missing (only to discover it under her bed) and when the dishes got smashed in the kitchen (not a burglary, but their resident stray cat who liked to sneak in the front door).

'It can't be a coincidence,' said Libby. 'People don't go around arguing with strangers. I wonder if this is connected to that letter she received?'

'That's a bit of a leap, even for you.'

'Did I tell you about the first time I met Miss Browne?' She told Connie about Miss Browne on the train, how keen she had been to keep hold of her red suitcase, not wanting anyone to touch it.

'Now I think of it, her suitcase...' Libby paused. 'Well, it looked just like yours!'

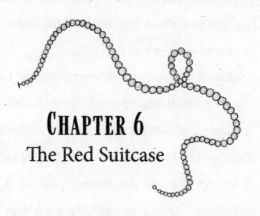

# CHAPTER 6
## The Red Suitcase

'I still don't understand why me and Miss Browne having the same type of suitcase is so interesting,' said Connie. 'There must be thousands of them. It's just a coincidence.'

'Urgh,' groaned Libby. 'You really have no imagination, Connie.'

Libby was exhausted after being dragged round the Louvre all day and the walk home seemed to be taking forever. Sebastian and Noah were just ahead, chattering noisily to Miss Browne. They were still full of energy.

Libby looked towards the school further down the

street and noticed a light coming from their room. The light seemed to move around – it came close to the window, then suddenly went out. She rubbed her eyes. Maybe she'd imagined it.

'Stop daydreaming.' Connie shook Libby's arm. 'I'll race you home.'

Connie ran ahead, with Libby in close pursuit. As they neared the school, a tall man came out of the door and hurried down the street in the opposite direction. Libby noticed the man was wearing a spotted bow tie.

They ran in and clattered noisily up the stairs, ignoring Miss Mousedale calling to them to slow down. Connie reached their floor first and declared herself the winner.

Libby paused. Their door was wide open. She was usually careful to close it before she went out, to stop the stray cat getting in and leaving her presents of dead mice.

'Did you leave the door open?' Libby asked, checking her bed for half-eaten rodents.

'I can't remember. It was such a rush this morning,'

replied Connie. They both had a bad habit of oversleeping. Too much reading by torchlight or chatting away meant that they always went to bed much later than they should.

The room was freezing cold. The window hadn't been closed properly. Pushing it shut, she peered down at the street below, looking to see if anyone was lurking about, but the road was so busy, it was difficult to tell.

'Shall we have some marshmallows on our hot chocolate?' asked Connie, 'I've got a secret stash under my bed.'

'Oooh, yes,' said Libby, easily distracted by the promise of sweets.

Connie's godmother sent the best tuck-boxes. They were stuffed with treats that they couldn't get in Paris: toffee bonbons, flying saucers, lollies that stuck your teeth together and sweet necklaces. But they weren't really supposed to keep food in their room, so Connie hid hers in her suitcase.

'And maybe some of that chocolate you've been saving?'

'As well?' laughed Connie. She took the key from the top drawer of her bedside cabinet and went to her wardrobe. 'That's strange. My suitcase is unlocked.'

'Really? Has someone been in it?' said Libby.

'Not likely,' said Connie. 'Weird, though. I always lock it.'

'Is anything missing?'

'Not sure.' Connie searched through her case. 'Oh no! My jewellery box has gone.' She emptied everything on to her bed to double-check.

'What was in it?'

'A locket that my grandmother gave me before she died,' Connie replied. 'And I think Mum packed my pearls.'

'Pearls? Why would your mum pack pearls?'

'She thinks a *lady* should never go anywhere without her pearls,' said Connie.

'Seriously?' asked Libby. 'What century does she live in?'

Connie flushed. 'Forget I said anything.' She put the pile of clothes back in her suitcase neatly and checked under the bed.

Libby looked at all the things in Connie's case. There was so much stuff in there. She'd never seen Connie wear any of it. She spotted something silver caught up in a scarf and carefully untangled it. 'Is this it?' she asked, holding up a silver locket engraved with a thistle.

'Yes!' Connie clapped her hands together. Her face lit up briefly and then she frowned and started rummaging through things again. 'But where are my pearls and jewellery box? Mum will be furious if I've lost them.' She started chewing her nails.

'I'm sure it will turn up. Don't worry. It's not like they're real, is it?' said Libby. Connie still looked upset. Libby put her arm around her. 'Let's have some hot chocolate.'

In the dining room, Sebastian and Noah were arguing as per usual. This time it was over a game of chess.

'Stop cheating! You know that move's not allowed.' Sebastian prodded his brother.

'Yes it is, you're just a bad loser.' Noah shoved him back.

Libby wondered if Noah had been playing one of his practical jokes. She couldn't stop herself from saying, 'Noah, have you been in our room?'

'Why would I go in your room?' asked Noah.

'Boys are strictly forbidden on the girl's floor,' he said, mimicking their headmistress.

'You sound exactly like Miss Mousedale,' laughed Sebastian. 'Good job she didn't hear you!'

Noah glanced over at Miss Mousedale in the corner. 'I'd be in huge trouble, if I got caught.' He winked at Libby.

'He's telling the truth – for a change,' said Sebastian. 'We came straight in here to finish our game.'

Connie's eyes were all red. Libby could see she was really upset about the missing pearls. *If it wasn't Noah, who else could it be?* 'Well, someone's gone through her things,' she said.

'Why are you accusing us?' said Noah. 'Only you two have been up there.'

'Some valuables have been stolen from Connie's suitcase.' Libby ignored the glares Connie was giving her.

'Libby,' hissed Connie. 'You can't go round saying someone has taken them.'

Miss Browne appeared behind them. 'What's this? Something's been stolen?'

'It's nothing,' said Connie, rubbing her eyes. 'Libby's just making a fuss.'

'It's not nothing,' said Libby. 'Connie's pearl necklace and jewellery box have gone missing.'

'Are you sure?' Miss Browne asked. 'Have you checked everywhere?'

Connie nodded. 'Libby thinks someone broke in, but nobody knows what's in my suitcase.'

'Your suitcase? They've been taken from *your* suitcase?' Miss Browne repeated.

Libby stared at Connie, as Miss Browne stormed up the stairs. 'You'd think it was her jewellery that's been stolen.'

They followed her back up to their room. Miss Browne had pulled out Connie's drawers and was rifling through them, making a huge mess.

'Where did you say you saw them last?' she demanded.

'I keep them in here.' Connie pulled out her suitcase. 'The pearls were in my jewellery box yesterday, when I put my earrings away.'

Miss Browne muttered to herself. 'It's red... That's

too much of a coincidence.'

Libby couldn't understand why Miss Browne was so fascinated by Connie's suitcase. *What does she mean, it's too much of a coincidence?* Although Libby had thought it was strange that Miss Browne and Connie had the same type of case, she hadn't expected Miss Browne to think the same!

Miss Browne took a step back. She caught her foot on the edge of the rug and nearly slipped.

'What's this?' she said, pulling out a string of iridescent beads with an ornate clasp from under the rug.

'My pearls,' said Connie, and her eyes lit up. 'Thank goodness for that!'

'But why were they on the floor?' asked Libby. 'I thought you'd locked them away.'

The strange look on Miss Browne's face disappeared, Libby noticed.

'So no one has broken in after all. You girls have such wild imaginations.'

Libby wanted to say that the jewellery box was still missing, but she thought it would just annoy

her teacher even more.

Miss Browne sighed. 'After all that excitement, I think I'll have an early night.'

Libby looked at the clock on her bedside table. It was only eight. That really was early!

'Goodnight. And thanks for helping,' said Connie.

Libby's mind was whirring with questions. Nothing seemed to add up. Despite Miss Browne's reassurances, she knew someone had to have been in their room. She remembered the mysterious light she'd seen in the bedroom window and the strange man she'd spotted leaving the school. Something was definitely going on!

# CHAPTER 7
## Montmartre

Connie didn't want to believe that anyone could have broken in, even though her jewellery box was still missing. She refused to talk about it and Libby didn't want to unsettle her any further. But Libby noticed that Connie always double-checked she'd locked her case whenever they went out for the day.

Miss Mousedale was determined they would explore as much of Paris as possible during their stay. She was fond of organising surprise trips and springing it on them at breakfast.

'We're off to Montmartre to do some more sketching and to visit the museum,' announced

Miss Mousedale. 'Make sure you pack your sketch pads and pencils.'

'You know what that means?' Libby groaned.

'What?' asked Connie.

'More steps to climb up.' Her legs still ached from walking up the Eiffel Tower yesterday.

One of the other teachers, Miss Wall, overheard her complaining. 'Come on, Libby, some fresh air and exercise will do you the world of good.'

'Yes, Miss Wall.' She found it hard not to giggle when she talked to Miss Wall. Her hair was a very bright shade of pink and piled up on the top of her head. It reminded Libby of a giant candyfloss.

'It's okay for her. She took the lift. Who knew school could be so exhausting!' Libby lowered her voice to a whisper. 'But don't worry, I know the best place for a hot chocolate and a croissant.'

'Is that all you ever think about? Food!' Connie laughed.

Libby stuck out her tongue at Connie, who pulled a face right back. They giggled as they wrapped up in their scarves and hats.

At the top of Montmartre, Libby looked at the view and smiled. Maybe it was worth the walk. From here, it felt like you could see across the whole of Paris.

The teachers had all taken the funicular up, so they weren't out of breath. Miss Mousedale led them to the square and gathered them all together.

'Sebastian, Noah, do pay attention and stop wandering off,' she said.

The twins were distracted by a man pretending to be a statue. He obviously wasn't that convincing; his hat was empty apart from one euro, a few cents and what looked like a button.

'Before we go into the museum, I want you to spend an hour using the street artists for inspiration. Look at the views they paint. Think about what you would sketch.'

'And remember, don't go too far from here, I don't want anyone getting lost.' Miss Browne smiled.

Libby wondered if she and Connie could manage to sneak off to the café. She saw the teachers all huddled together and listened in.

Miss Browne pointed to a street off the square and

said, 'Do come, Miss Mousedale, I really could do with your help.'

Libby wondered what Miss Browne wanted her aunt for. It would be much easier to escape if there was only Miss Wall watching them.

'If you insist, but we can't be too long.' Miss Mousedale turned to Miss Wall. 'Will you be okay on your own?'

Before she could hear Miss Wall's answer, Connie nudged Libby. 'C'mon, let's go find a good spot!'

The Place du Tertre was scattered with artists painting. Libby and Connie walked around, peering over their shoulders. Most of them had chosen the obvious Parisian landmarks: the Eiffel Tower, the Sacré-Cœur and the Arc de Triomphe.

'You could do better than some of these, Connie,' Libby whispered.

'I might sketch some people,' said Connie. 'That's more my style.'

Libby smiled. 'And I know the perfect place for people-watching. The café I was telling you about.'

Connie laughed. 'How did I know you were going to say that?'

Linking arms, they walked over the uneven cobbles to the café on the corner. Libby hoped Miss Wall wouldn't notice that she wasn't actually doing any work, unlike Connie, who was sketching the artists in the square. Libby wasn't in the mood to draw. Taking her camera out, she decided she could take some photos and maybe sketch them later. Then she wouldn't get into trouble!

Lifting up her camera, she adjusted the lens and started snapping anything that caught her eye: a young girl with a balloon, a man carrying a bunch of flowers, a tall lady striding across the square wearing a blue hat with a peacock feather. Libby wondered where she was going in such a hurry.

That hat looked familiar. She looked back at her photograph, studying it carefully. The woman looked a bit like the lady from the Louvre, although she'd only seen the back of her head. The hat looked exactly the same.

'Connie, look at this.' She passed the camera across.

'What am I looking at?'

'It's the same person we saw at the Louvre. I'm sure of it,' said Libby.

'What?'

'The one who was arguing with Miss Browne.'

Libby stared after the peacock feather, as the woman made her way down one of the winding streets and disappeared out of view.

'I didn't see her, remember?' said Connie. 'I was too busy sketching.'

Libby sighed. 'It's too late. I think we've lost her.'

'Why, what were you planning to do? Follow her?' laughed Connie.

Libby was fed up of nobody taking her seriously. 'What if I was? I never did find out what's going on with Miss Browne.'

'Don't be silly. This isn't one of your mystery books,' said Connie. 'I know she's been acting a bit odd, but that doesn't mean anything is going on.'

Libby sighed. *Why did Connie always have to be so reasonable?* She finished her drink and looked around. Noah was balancing along a high wall, wobbling dramatically. He didn't look very safe.

'Look what Noah's doing now,' Libby pointed.

Sebastian was trying to get Noah to come down off the wall but the more he tried, the more Noah fooled about.

'Ignore him, he's just showing off,' said Connie.

Noah wobbled again and took a step forward to balance. He let out a cry as his foot caught in a gap in the wall. He fell, landing awkwardly on the ground.

Sebastian yelled out and Miss Wall rushed over. Libby and Connie jumped up, grabbed their rucksacks and ran across the square. Miss Wall was trying to help Noah to get up, but he was clutching his arm and moaning.

'It really hurts,' Noah said. 'I think I'm going to be sick.' His face had turned green.

'Connie, fetch Miss Mousedale. I think we're going to have to take Noah to hospital.'

Connie looked round. 'But … I don't know where she is.'

'She went up that street,' said Libby, pointing.

'They were going to the jeweller's,' said Miss Wall. 'Quickly, go get her.'

Libby and Connie ran up the road. They didn't have to go too far before they spotted the only jeweller's in the street. A sign above the door in swirly, ornate writing said, 'Bijoutiers Deco'. The dark blue door had a sign: *Sur rendez-vous uniquement.*

*It looks very fancy,* thought Libby. *You even needed an appointment to get in! What could Miss Browne be looking for in here?*

'This must be it,' she said, peering into the window, which was filled with the most unusual and beautiful jewellery she'd ever seen in her life. There were rows of sparkling rings with large colourful stones glinting in the sunshine and an array of strange and wonderful brooches.

In the reflection in the glass, she thought she

spotted a peacock feather. She turned around, but there was nobody there. Perhaps her imagination was playing tricks on her?

'Libby, stop getting distracted,' complained Connie. 'I think we need to ring the bell to get in.'

A row of bikes were parked outside the shop. Stepping back, Libby tripped over something and fell into the nearest one. Like dominoes, all the bikes collapsed onto each other, making an almighty noise.

'Ooops!' Libby flushed.

The door flung open and a furious assistant appeared on the step. Libby could see Miss Browne standing behind her. Now she was in trouble.

*'Mon dieu. Qu'avez-vous fait?'* the woman shouted, waving her hands.

Libby wasn't quite sure what she'd said, but she was clearly cross. *'Pardonnez-moi,'* she stuttered. *'Je suis désolée!'*

'Libby, is that you?' Miss Browne stared at her.

Libby struggled to her feet. She could feel her face glowing. She tried to pick up the bicycles, but they were too heavy.

Miss Browne sighed. 'Oh, Libby, what have you done?'

'What's happened?' said Miss Mousedale, appearing behind Miss Browne.

Libby stuttered, 'Sorry, it's just Noah has had an accident and Miss Wall asked us to fetch you. I didn't mean to...'

'Come quickly,' Connie pleaded. 'We think he needs to go to hospital.'

'Miss Mousedale, we must go at once,' said Miss Browne.

Libby's aunt immediately headed off, running to where she'd left the class.

Miss Browne didn't move.

'Mademoiselle, must you go?' asked the assistant. 'Will you return?'

*Je ne sais pas,*' Miss Browne said. 'My friend said she'd got everything she was looking for.' She shrugged her shoulders, pointing after Miss Mousedale. 'I don't know why, but she seems to be in a great hurry.'

Libby thought that was a strange thing to say. Miss Browne knew exactly why her aunt was in such a rush. She thought she saw a smile flash across the teacher's face. What did she have to smile about?

# CHAPTER 8
## A Surprise Visitor

They were meant to be practising their French vocabulary but Libby had other things on her mind. Miss Wall was making them repeat their verbs over and over again. Libby sighed loudly, making everyone in the class turn round to look at her.

'Shhhh,' said Connie. 'You'll get us in trouble.'

'Elizabeth! Stop gossiping with Constance,' said Miss Wall, clearly exasperated.

Libby blushed. She knew they were in trouble when Miss Wall called them by their full names.

'*Pardonnez-moi*, Mademoiselle Wall.'

But when Miss Wall wasn't watching, she leaned

over again and whispered, 'I'm sure it was the same lady I saw at the Louvre.'

Connie glared at her. 'I'm trying to work… Okay, I believe you. Why does it matter?'

Libby sighed. She really tried to focus on her lesson but a stream of questions filled her head. Who was that lady with the hat? Was it the woman Miss Browne had been arguing with? It was too much of a coincidence. Miss Browne had told her that she didn't know anyone in Paris, but they kept seeing her with strangers.

At lunchtime, they all feasted on crusty bread and soft cheese. Libby thought the food in Paris had to be the best she'd had anywhere. She cut herself another generous slab of Brie and took a huge bite.

'I love the food here,' said Connie. 'We never get anything so tasty at home. Mrs MacCallum is a great cook but Dad always insists on such boring food.'

'Who's Mrs MacCallum?'

asked Libby, her mouth half full.

'Er … she's our cook,' said Connie.

'You've got your own cook? That's a bit fancy!'

Connie looked down at her lunch. 'It's just that my parents are terrible at cooking and … er … they even burn toast.'

Libby wasn't convinced that was a reason to have your very own cook. But something else was bugging her. 'Do you think that lady could have been following Miss Browne?'

'I don't know. Why would anyone follow her?' asked Connie. 'You do have the strangest ideas. Maybe they were intending to meet, but Noah's accident ruined her plans.'

'Okay,' said Libby begrudgingly. 'That would make sense, I suppose. Still doesn't explain why they were arguing at the Louvre.'

'Were they arguing though?' Connie said. 'You only saw them briefly. Can you really be sure?'

'I'm sure Miss Browne said she wasn't the person she was looking for. Don't you think that's a strange thing to say?' asked Libby.

Before Connie could answer, the doorbell rang. A moment later, the concierge appeared with an older man.

'A visitor for you, Mademoiselle Mousedale – Inspecteur de Villiers.'

Miss Mousedale lowered her glasses and looked up, clearly surprised. He took off his hat and showed her a card from his wallet.

'Inspecteur, how can I help you?' she asked.

'Apologies for the intrusion. I'm here on a delicate matter.' He looked around the room. 'Is there somewhere private we can talk?'

Libby looked at Connie. *What would an inspector want with her aunt?*

Miss Mousedale hesitated for a moment, then smiled. 'Of course, after you.' She gestured to the hall.

The door shut behind them, but then swung back open slightly, and Libby could just about see her aunt and the inspector talking. Miss Mousedale was shaking her head and looked flushed, but she couldn't hear what they were saying.

'Oooh, wonder what Miss Mousedale has done?'

laughed Noah. 'She must be in *big* trouble!'

'Yeah,' said Sebastian. '*Huge* trouble!'

Connie threw a cushion at the twins. 'Shut up, you two. She'll be back in a minute and *you'll* be the ones in trouble,' she warned.

'Don't be so boring, Connie. Can't you take a joke?' Sebastian grinned.

Libby was too embarrassed to say anything. Sometimes it was really tricky having her aunt as head teacher. She felt like all the other students were staring at her.

They both ignored Connie and carried on being silly. Libby walked over to close the dining-room door, so her aunt wouldn't hear them. She saw Miss Mousedale and the inspector talking at the bottom of the stairs and couldn't help eavesdropping.

'What's going on?' asked Connie, behind her.

Libby put her finger to her mouth. 'Ssshhh!'

'So you don't deny being in the shop when it happened?' asked the inspector. He handed a photo to Miss Mousedale.

'We were both in the shop,' said Miss Mousedale,

clearly flustered. 'You can see that in the photo but … how do you know it went missing when we were there?'

Libby was stunned. What had gone missing? Was her aunt in some sort of trouble? She felt embarrassed that Connie could hear.

'Apparently, you were alone for a few moments, giving you the perfect opportunity to take the brooch. Then you left the shop very quickly,' accused the inspector.

'There was an emergency. Neither myself nor Louisa are thieves!' She hesitated. 'Search our rooms, if you don't believe me.'

He tipped his hat. 'Oh, we will! I have the *mandat de perquisition* with me.' He opened the front door. A *gendarme* was waiting.

Libby gasped. This couldn't be happening. Her aunt wasn't a thief!

'If you could show him where your rooms are, we'll start there,' said the inspector. 'I can assure you, madame, we will get to the bottom of this.'

Libby silently closed the door and turned to Connie.

Her heart was beating so loudly she could hear it.

'I don't understand,' whispered Connie.

Libby saw Noah staring outside. He said, 'There's a police car out there. Oooh, have they come to take Miss Mousedale away?'

Libby tried to ignore him. 'She was only in the shop on her own for a moment,' she said to Connie.

'There must be some kind of mistake,' said Connie. 'Why would she steal a brooch?'

'Of course she hasn't stolen anything,' snapped Libby, her eyes stinging with tears. 'How could you think that?'

'Sorry...' Connie stuttered. 'It's just...'

'Well, they won't find anything.' Libby could feel everyone staring at her. 'They'll have to admit they've made a terrible mistake.'

The door opened and Miss Wall came in. 'Miss Mousedale has a visitor,' she said. 'I think we'll go and get some fresh air. Quickly, finish your lunches.'

Libby had lost her appetite. She put the rest of her food in the bin. She could see the other students whispering and she could guess what they were talking about.

'It'll be fine, Libby, don't worry,' said Connie, as they crossed the road and headed towards the Parc du Champ-de-Mars. 'I'm sure Miss Browne will back up your aunt.'

As usual, the park was busy with tourists, so it was easy for Libby and Connie to drop behind and talk without being overheard. Libby was shocked. Despite Connie's reassurances, she wasn't convinced it would all be fine. The inspector must have some evidence. He wouldn't just turn up with a search warrant unless he had some proof that her aunt was involved.

'Do you think this could be linked to the break-in?' asked Libby. 'First your jewellery box goes missing, now this brooch.'

'I don't know. I'm still not convinced someone stole my jewellery box,' said Connie. 'Why would they take that and leave behind the jewellery?'

'Maybe the thief dropped them, they were by the window,' Libby said. 'Or they realised your pearls weren't worth stealing. It's not as if they're real.'

Connie flushed. 'Er … they are, though. They're kind of a family heirloom.'

Before Libby could react, Miss Wall called them all together. 'Let's head back,' she said. 'It's getting dark.'

Libby shivered. The sky had dimmed and the sun had completely disappeared. As they neared the school, Libby could see that the *gendarme's* car was still parked outside.

'Connie, look, it's still here. Maybe they haven't found anything?'

Just then, the door opened and Miss Mousedale and the inspector came out. He was carrying a clear bag which looked as if it had some photos inside.

Miss Browne stood in the doorway. To Libby, it looked as if she was smiling. But Libby forgot about the other teacher when she realised her aunt was wearing handcuffs. She watched in disbelief as Miss Mousedale was led to the waiting car by the *gendarme*.

Horrified, she rushed over. 'Let her go! There must be a mistake,' she shouted.

'I'll be back in no time, Libby,

don't worry. I'm sure it's just a misunderstanding.'
Libby could see the confusion in her aunt's eyes.

As the car drove away, Libby burst into tears. She'd always wanted to be involved in her very own mystery, but now it was real, she desperately wished she wasn't.

# CHAPTER 9
## A Terrible Mistake

Libby stared at her dinner plate. She usually loved *frites* but tonight every single one stuck in her throat. It felt as if all the other students were whispering about her. She kept hoping the inspector would realise his mistake and bring her aunt home.

'I'm not hungry.' She pushed her plate away and stood up.

'Wait,' said Connie. 'I'm nearly done.'

'I can't…' Her eyes blurred. Libby ran out of the room.

Lying under her duvet, she replayed the day over and over in her head – holding the worn patch at the tip of Bonnie's ear. It didn't make any sense. What was she going to tell her mum? She would be horrified. Libby desperately wanted to talk to her. If only she could hear her voice for a few minutes.

The bedroom door creaked open and Libby heard footsteps moving quietly across the floor.

'Are you asleep?' whispered Connie.

Libby wiped her face. It felt red and hot. She didn't want Connie to know she'd been crying.

'No, I just couldn't face anyone.' She pulled the duvet off her head.

'I'm really sorry. I'm sure it's just a horrible misunderstanding and she'll be home soon.' Connie sat at the end of the bed.

Libby didn't know what to say. All her thoughts were whirring around her head. She needed to prove her aunt was innocent, but where should she start?

'I just don't believe she's capable of stealing. There must be some other explanation,' she insisted.

'I don't think she took it either. Don't worry, we'll work it out.' Connie reached over and hugged Libby.

'I've got an idea!' Connie went to her bedside table

and got out her notebook. 'Let's take some inspiration from those *Isobel Investigates* books you're always reading and write down everything we know. Isn't that what she usually does?'

Libby frowned. 'I know you're trying to help, but I've got a horrible headache.'

'Firstly, we need to return to the scene of the crime to see if we can spot any obvious clues,' said Connie, ignoring Libby. 'Why did they go to the jeweller's?'

Libby sat up. 'I heard Miss Browne ask my aunt to help her. Something about choosing a present.'

'A present?' asked Connie. 'It's the sort of place my mum would shop at. Everything looked very expensive!'

'I don't know, maybe she just enjoys looking at nice things.' Libby liked to gaze into the windows of patisseries, admiring the rainbows of macarons on display, even if she couldn't always buy them.

'All right,' said Connie. 'If it wasn't her idea, Miss Mousedale can't have planned to steal the brooch.'

'True,' said Libby. 'But that's hardly proof.'

Connie scribbled something in her notebook.

'What else do we know?'

'They're convinced the brooch disappeared when they were in the shop,' said Libby. 'But how could either of them have stolen it without being spotted?'

Thinking about it logically made Libby feel better. If they could put together the pieces of the puzzle, maybe it could help clear her aunt's name.

'They would need an opportunity or a distraction,' said Connie. She circled 'opportunity' in her notebook.

'What kind?' asked Libby. Her thoughts were in a jumble.

'The bicycles!' they both said at the same time.

Libby blushed. Had she caused all this trouble when she knocked the bicycles over?

'Then it definitely can't have been planned,' she said. 'There's no way they could have known I was going to knock over the bikes.'

'True. But the police don't know that.'

'Do you think the police suspect me?' Libby was horrified. 'She is my aunt.'

'Don't be silly,' said Connie. 'The inspector would have spoken to you by now if you were a suspect.'

Libby couldn't believe it; just as she'd thought it couldn't get any worse, it looked as if she could be mixed up in the theft.

'It definitely doesn't sound planned,' agreed Connie. 'If it wasn't for you, there wouldn't have been any distraction.'

'Oh, thanks!'

Did Connie think she was involved? She couldn't bear it!

'There is another obvious suspect,' said Connie. 'Miss Browne.'

'The inspector said my aunt was the only one alone in the shop.' Libby remembered. 'Miss Browne came out right behind the shop assistant.'

She could see why the inspector had arrested her aunt and not Miss Browne. She pictured the clear bag the inspector had been carrying when he left the school. *What had been in there?*

'I can't bear this,' said Libby. 'I can't just sit here and do nothing!'

Connie looked worried. 'Please tell me you're not going to do anything stupid or dangerous?'

'I want to look in my aunt's room. I'll feel better just by being there and I might find something that will explain what's going on.'

Connie hesitated. 'I don't know, Libby. What if you get caught?'

'I'll just say I thought the stray cat had got locked in there and I was letting him out.'

'Well, if you're going, I'm coming with you,' said Connie. 'And if anyone catches us, you're going to do the explaining!'

'Thanks,' said Libby, wiping her eyes and throwing her arms around Connie. 'Grab your torch. I don't want to turn the light on in case someone sees.' She crossed the hall and went to the top of the stairs. 'Come on.' She beckoned.

'I just need to do something.' Connie dashed back into the room. She came out a few moments later and followed Libby down the stairs.

They tiptoed down, trying to avoid the creaky stair. Libby hesitated outside the door. She knew it was wrong to go into her aunt's room without permission, but she didn't know what else to do. Libby nudged the door open. She couldn't believe the mess the room was in. Drawers hung open and there were clothes thrown on the bed. Her aunt would be horrified.

'We can't leave it like this.'

Both girls started tidying, putting things back in cupboards and on shelves.

Libby opened the wardrobe and found her aunt's suitcase. She could feel her heart beating in her chest as she put it straight, knowing her aunt would be really upset about her going through her things. Underneath some scarves she spotted a box. She couldn't see it clearly as the only light was from the street light outside.

'Connie, pass me your torch.'

Connie threw it to her and she shone the light over the box. It had a thistle engraved on the top. She knew thistles were a symbol of Scotland. Was this Connie's jewellery box? Why would her aunt have taken it?

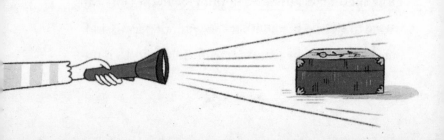

Libby quickly put the jewellery box back in the suitcase and closed the wardrobe door. She couldn't bring herself to tell Connie.

'Libby, look at this.' Connie held up a photo of some girls wearing school uniform and sitting under a tree.

'I guess they must be her school friends,' said Libby. Her aunt looked so happy. Libby remembered how sad she'd been this afternoon. Her heart sank. She needed to find a way to help her.

Connie studied the photo. 'I think that's my mum.

I wonder who the other girls are?' said Connie.

'Really?' said Libby. 'I forgot they went to school together.'

They heard footsteps on the stairs. Libby turned off the torch and stood completely still.

'That must be Miss Wall for lights out,' she whispered. 'She's going to be mad when she realises we're not in our room.'

'Five minutes' warning, girls,' called Miss Wall.

Things were going from bad to worse. Libby was sure she heard their door open upstairs. They were about to get caught. She doubted Miss Wall would believe her story of looking for the cat.

'Already fast asleep,' murmured Miss Wall. She switched off the hall light and went back down the stairs. Libby held her breath as footsteps went past the door. After a few minutes she heard the sound of the running tap from the bathroom across the hall.

Libby was completely confused. 'How did…?'

Connie smiled. 'I put some pillows under our duvets to make it look as if we were sleeping. Didn't think we would actually get away with it.'

'Quick, let's get back upstairs before Miss Wall catches us,' said Libby.

Libby was so relieved that they had not been caught. But she was no closer to proving her aunt's innocence. Finding Connie's jewellery box was making Libby doubt herself. She couldn't think of any reason for it being in her aunt's room, unless she had stolen it. Did this mean her aunt was guilty of stealing the brooch too?

She needed to find out exactly what had happened at the jeweller's.

# CHAPTER 10
## A Lady in Waiting

The next morning Libby woke with a terrible headache. For one moment she'd totally forgotten what had happened the day before. And then she remembered.

With a sinking feeling in her stomach, she realised she didn't really know if her aunt was guilty or not. How could she find out the truth?

Getting up and opening the curtains, she saw a lady wearing a black-and-white coat sitting on the bench in front of the *boulangerie* opposite, reading a newspaper. Libby couldn't see her face clearly as she was wearing sunglasses, even though it was dull outside.

She looked over at Connie, who was still fast asleep, and checked her clock. It was almost nine o'clock and breakfast would nearly be over.

'Connie, wake up,' she shouted. 'We've overslept.'

'Urrghh,' groaned Connie, rolling out of bed.

'Come on, sleepyhead,' said Libby.

They got dressed and headed downstairs. The dining room was almost empty. Libby knew they must be really late. There was only Miss Browne and a few of the older students sitting at the table.

'Morning, Libby, did you sleep well?' asked Miss Browne as Libby sat down next to her.

'Yes.' She tried to smile but couldn't manage it. It seemed unfair that only her aunt had been arrested and not Miss Browne. Surely both of them had had the chance to commit the crime – they were in the jeweller's together? How could the inspector be so sure it was her aunt? She knew her aunt had been on her own for a moment, but that couldn't be the only reason they had arrested her.

'I've spoken to your aunt this morning. She's fine.' Miss Browne put her arm around Libby's shoulders. 'Hopefully she'll be home any day.'

'Are they letting her go?' Libby's heart leaped. That must mean she wasn't guilty. She felt terrible for even suspecting her aunt.

'Well, no, not exactly. But while she's away she's asked me to step in as head teacher,' said Miss Browne.

'Why?' said Libby. 'If she's coming back soon.'

'It's a bit complicated,' said Miss Browne. 'Nothing for you to worry about.'

Libby was even more confused. *Did this mean they were charging her aunt with the theft?*

'What happened in the jeweller's?' asked Libby. 'Why do they think she took the brooch?'

Miss Browne flushed. 'Try not to think about that,' she insisted. 'Leave the inspector to do his job.'

Libby didn't agree. If the inspector was doing his job properly then he wouldn't have arrested her aunt. Unless he had some proof her aunt was guilty. She knew Miss Browne was trying to be kind, but that wasn't going to help them solve this puzzle.

'Why did you go to the jeweller's?' asked Connie.

Miss Browne's smile didn't quite reach her eyes. 'Really, girls, what is it with all these questions? If you must know, your aunt wanted my help choosing a present.'

Libby looked across at Connie and saw her reaction. They both knew that was a lie.

'Finish your breakfast,' said Miss Browne, quickly changing the subject. 'We're off to the Pompidou Centre in ten minutes.'

Libby was frustrated. For most of the night, she'd been awake, staring at the ceiling, wondering what would happen to her if her aunt was found guilty.

Connie whispered, 'I can't believe Miss Browne is lying!'

Libby nodded. 'I know! She must be hiding something.'

'Or,' said Connie, 'she's worried that if the inspector knew it was her idea to go to the jeweller's, he might start questioning her.'

'I don't believe either of them could be the thief,'

said Libby. 'Maybe the assistant at the shop is lying?' She rubbed her still aching head.

'How can we find out?' said Connie.

\*\*\*

When they went outside onto the street, Libby noticed the lady in the black-and-white coat was still sitting on the bench.

'Hurry up, girls,' shouted Miss Wall. 'We don't want to leave you behind.'

The métro was busy. Libby and Connie were squashed together right at the end, away from the rest of the group. It was only two stops to Rambuteau, luckily, so they wouldn't have to stand for too long.

'We need to go back to that jeweller's and ask the assistant some questions,' said Libby. 'The only problem is I don't think they'll let us in. That sign said "by appointment only". And I doubt they'll give a couple of schoolgirls an appointment.'

Connie smiled. 'I've been thinking and I might have a way to get round that. There's something I haven't told you. But you must promise not to tell anyone else!'

'Go on,' said Libby, intrigued. The carriage swayed from side to side and they grabbed hold of the rails.

'I'm not telling you until you promise,' insisted Connie.

Libby rolled her eyes and held up her finger. 'Fine. Pinky promise.' She locked fingers with Connie.

'They might not let us in, but I'm sure they'll let in the daughter of the Earl of Laithness,' whispered Connie.

'That's not helpful,' moaned Libby. 'How are we going to get his daughter to come with us?'

Connie looked around the carriage to check no one could hear her. 'It's a bit embarrassing. But my father is an earl, which makes me a lady. You're looking at Lady Constance Montgomery!'

'Yeah, good one,' said Libby. 'I'm not in the mood for jokes.'

'I'm not joking,' said Connie. 'It's nothing really, just an old family name and I never use it. But if it helps us get in, I will. As long as you don't tell anyone!'

Libby smiled. 'Oh, now it makes sense,' she smiled. 'No wonder you've got "family heirlooms" to bring to school.'

'It's just a set of pearls.' Connie blushed. 'But remember, you swore not to tell!'

'Okay, calm down,' laughed Libby. 'You know this might actually work. We just need to find a way to go there on our own.'

The train slammed to a halt. 'It's our stop,' said Connie. 'Quick, before we miss it.'

Outside, it had started to rain. Miss Wall and Miss Browne ushered them quickly to the Pompidou Centre, so they wouldn't get completely soaked.

'My class,' said Miss Browne, 'we're going to the library to do some research on your favourite Parisian landmark for your projects.'

Noah groaned and rolled his eyes. 'Boring!'

'Stop moaning,' snapped Libby. She didn't like seeing Miss Browne taking charge when it should be her aunt organising them all.

'Sorry, Libby,' said Sebastian, pulling Noah to one side.

Libby could hear Noah muttering and Sebastian trying to distract him. They headed into the library and Connie steered Libby in the opposite direction away from the twins. 'There are two computers free over here,' said Connie.

Libby just stared at the screen. She wasn't in the mood to work, unlike Connie, who was completely focused, tapping away at the keyboard, clearly on a mission to get her work done.

'Connie, you're a bit keen,' Libby sighed. 'I can't think. My brain hurts.'

Connie looked up and smiled. 'I thought this would be the perfect opportunity to do some other research.' She turned the screen around so Libby could see it.

'Is that what I think it is?' Libby leaned over to take a closer look.

'Yes! I searched for anything about the theft in the news.'

Libby scanned the article. It didn't include a lot of details, just that a theft had taken place and someone had been taken into custody. Underneath was a photo of an enormous heart-shaped brooch with two large green jewels and an even bigger red jewel in the centre.

'It says they haven't recovered the jewel. So they can't have found it in Miss Mousedale's room,' said Connie.

Libby breathed a sigh of relief. 'Then why have they arrested her? They must have some other evidence.' She paused. 'I know they took something away in a clear bag but I couldn't see properly what it was. It looked like some photos.'

'It doesn't say what evidence they have,' said Connie. 'This is good news. It means they can't know for sure she did it.'

Across the desks, Libby saw a woman at a computer opposite lean forward. It could just be her imagination, but it looked as if she was trying to listen to their conversation.

She lowered her voice, just in case. 'Where can the brooch be? I can't believe anyone would steal it. It's so ugly.'

'It's probably worth a fortune. My mum has a necklace with large jewels like this, but it's always locked away in the safe. She only wears it for balls and parties,' said Connie.

Libby stared at her. 'Balls? I forgot I was in the presence of a lady.' She laughed loudly.

'Shhh,' said Connie. 'I told you I don't want anyone else finding out. It was really embarrassing at my last school. They all thought I was really stuck up.'

'Sorry,' said Libby. 'It must have been awful for you.'

The woman opposite stood up and hurried out of the library. Her black-and-white coat swished behind her.

Libby stared at the brooch. If only they could find it, that would prove her aunt was innocent. But what hope did they have? Something about this whole mess wasn't quite right. Libby needed to think it through.

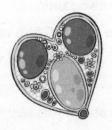

# CHAPTER 11
## In the Dead of the Night

By the time they got back from the Pompidou Centre, Libby was worn out. She'd struggled to concentrate all day and had been told off twice in the museum for not listening. As they headed down the road to the school, Libby saw the light was on in her aunt's bedroom.

'I think my aunt is back!' She ran towards the entrance and flew through the door, straight to her aunt's room. Libby forced herself to stop and knock gently in case she was sleeping. She knew her aunt would be worn out after being stuck at the police station.

'Aunt Agatha, are you awake?'

She heard footsteps and her aunt opened the door. 'Libby, I'm so happy to see you, come in.'

Libby flung her arms round her and hugged her tightly, tears rolling down her face. After a few moments, Miss Mousedale closed the door and gestured for Libby to sit on the chair by her dressing table. Libby wiped away her tears, embarrassed. She was glad they'd tidied up the room before she got home. It looked like the *gendarme* had never been in here.

'I don't believe you took it, not one bit. And I'm going to prove you're innocent,' garbled Libby.

Any doubts she'd had about her aunt's innocence disappeared the moment she saw her face. She could see the dark circles under her eyes that hadn't been there before and the worry lines etched into her forehead.

'Oh, Libby,' Miss Mousedale smiled. 'You mustn't worry. I'm home, that's the main thing.'

'But what about the brooch?' asked Libby. 'They didn't find it, so how can they blame you.'

'It's a bit more complicated than that. They found some things that make them think I'm guilty.' She paused. 'I'm not sure how the things got into my room. I didn't put them there.'

'What did they find?'

Had someone planted evidence in her aunt's room? She knew Connie would think that was far-fetched, but how else could they be there?

'It is very strange,' said Miss Mousedale. 'Apparently they found a photo of the stolen brooch and some equipment which they claim I used to disable the CCTV.'

'The CCTV was disabled?' Libby was shocked. 'But that doesn't prove you stole the brooch!'

'Well, the inspector thinks I'm guilty. He even said I'd made the appointment at the jeweller's.' Miss Mousedale sighed. 'Until this is all cleared up I will have to let Miss Browne look after the school. I can't be in charge with this accusation hanging over me.'

Libby could see her aunt was getting upset. She needed to stop asking questions for now. 'I'm so glad you're home. Shall I make you a hot drink?'

'Let's go and make one together. I can't hide away in here all night,' said Miss Mousedale, smiling.

Libby could tell her aunt was trying to be brave. It wasn't her usual cheerful smile and it gave Libby a glimpse of how she was truly feeling.

In the dining room, Connie was chatting to Sebastian and Noah while Miss Browne read a book. They all looked up.

'You're back,' gasped Miss Browne. 'I mean, I'm so happy you're home.'

Miss Browne looked genuinely surprised to see Libby's aunt, despite all of her earlier reassurances.

'I am … for now, anyway,' said Miss Mousedale, sitting next to her at the window.

The room was unnaturally silent. Libby wished someone would say something. She looked over at Connie and tried to smile.

'Who wants a game of Scrabble?' asked Connie.

'Me,' said Libby and Sebastian at the same time. Libby went to the cupboard and got out the game.

'Not me, it's so dull,' groaned Noah.

Libby listened to her aunt and Miss Browne

chatting quietly. She could hear the odd word like 'passport', and 'police station', but that was all.

'Libby, it's your go,' said Connie, nudging her.

She stared at the letters in front of her: she had one vowel and far too many consonants, including a 'Z'. If only she could find a way to play that. The only spare vowel on the board was an 'A'. She had an idea and put down her letters. 'Zebra,' she proclaimed. 'And on a double-word score.'

'Good one,' said Connie, scribbling down Libby's score.

'Hang on.' Libby paused. 'Zebra – now I remember.'

Connie looked puzzled. 'What do you remember about a zebra?'

'Nothing,' said Libby. 'I was just thinking out loud.'

She had remembered why she recognised the black-and-white coat the woman was wearing in the library. It had reminded her of a zebra with its stripy print. It was exactly like the coat the other woman had worn sitting outside the school. What if they were the same woman?

Libby tried to carry on with the game, but all she

could think about was the woman with the black-and-white coat. Was she following them? Why? Was it the police watching her, thinking she was part of the robbery? She knew it looked really suspicious that she was outside the jeweller's when the brooch was stolen. After all, she had caused the distraction. Maybe they even thought she'd disabled the CCTV. Her heart beat wildly.

The dining room quickly filled up. Libby found it difficult to think with so much noise around her. It felt good to have her aunt back. Hopefully this would stop everyone speculating about the theft. She even laughed – somewhat reluctantly – at one of Noah's terrible impressions. Maybe it would all be okay, if she could just figure out what was going on.

'I think I'm going to have an early night,' said Miss Mousedale.

Libby yawned. 'Me too, I'm exhausted.'

Connie looked at the clock. 'I need to finish my drink and then I'll be up.'

Libby went upstairs, changed into her pyjamas and brushed her teeth. She hoped Connie would come to bed soon, so she could tell her she might be being followed. Her feet felt like ice. She climbed into bed, snuggled under her duvet and yawned again. *I'm just going to close my eyes for a minute,* she thought.

\*\*\*

When Libby woke up, the room was in complete darkness. Connie was fast asleep. Libby checked the time on her clock: it was just after one o'clock. She heard a yowling noise outside. *I bet it's that stray cat again,* she thought. *He's probably trying to get back into school to find a warm spot to sleep in.* Maybe his screeching had woken her up.

She shivered as she padded over to open the window to check. Looking outside, she started, as a light flashed on and off. Ducking back, she searched up and down until she spotted a figure hidden in the shadows by the lamp post.

'Connie,' she whispered.

Connie didn't stir.

She went over and roughly shook her. 'Wake up!'

Connie jumped up. 'What?' She looked at her clock. 'It's the middle of the night!'

Libby put her finger to her lips. 'Never mind, come here.' She beckoned her over and pointed to the figure below. 'Look.'

Connie shrugged. 'So?' She rubbed her eyes. 'Is that what you woke me up for?'

'Someone is lurking outside the school! I saw them signal with a light, on and off.'

'I'm too tired to care,' Connie yawned. 'Go back to bed, Libby.'

They both heard a noise and looked down. The school's front door opened beneath them. Someone crossed the street to the shadowy figure. The light from the lamp post illuminated their face just long enough for Libby and Connie to see who it was.

'Miss Browne!' said Libby. 'Why is she sneaking out of the school in the middle of the night?'

'That is strange,' Connie agreed.

Watching carefully, Libby could see the figure hand over a parcel to Miss Browne. She opened it up and took out what looked like a small box but Libby was too far away to see what was inside. The other person – Libby could see now it was a man – headed off into the darkness.

Miss Browne glanced around and then headed back inside, as she got closer Libby could see that she was smiling.

'Before you say anything, Connie, this can't be a coincidence!'

'No, you're right. Something odd is going on,' said Connie yawning. She smiled. 'Now can I go back to bed?'

Libby nodded, but muttered to herself, 'I am going to work out exactly what she's up to!'

# CHAPTER 12
## A Cat in the Attic

'I need to get in Miss Browne's room,' said Libby. She hadn't slept well and as soon as light began to flood the room, she leaped out of bed and shook Connie awake.

Connie yawned. 'Not again! Go back to bed.'

'No time for sleep. I've got to find out what was in that box!'

'I know,' yawned Connie again, 'but can't it wait for another hour?' She pulled her duvet over her head.

'No,' insisted Libby. 'We need to prove my aunt is innocent!'

Connie sat up. 'Fine, I give up. What's your plan?'

Libby sat on the bed and thought. The box was most likely to be in Miss Browne's room.

'I know – I'll offer to help Madame Roux clean the rooms,' said Libby.

'What? You're the messiest person I know. There's no way she'll let you,' said Connie. 'It will look really suspicious!'

'How about I'll pretend to be ill and when you all go out, I'll stay in and can search her room?'

'That might work. But what if you get caught?'

'I'll just have to make sure I'm not. I think everyone is going out today,' insisted Libby.

'Fine. What do you need me to do?'

'Tell Miss Wall I'm sick. And try to find a way to keep them out as long as possible,' pleaded Libby.

'I'll do my best,' said Connie. 'But we're not supposed to be going far today. Just a quick visit to the Arc de Triomphe.'

'That should give me enough time. I'm sure the box is linked somehow to the theft. The sooner I find it, the sooner I can work out what's going on,' said Libby.

 126

She jumped back into bed and started groaning.

'You're going to have to try harder than that,' laughed Connie. 'It's not very convincing.'

*** 

When Libby heard the door slam, she knew she'd have to act fast. Connie hadn't been able to find out about the older students' plans, so she had no idea how long they'd be out. But all she had to do was find this mysterious box and see what was inside. How difficult could it be?

Dashing across the landing, she inched Miss Browne's door open and paused. What if she was just jumping to conclusions about Miss Browne and this was all perfectly innocent? No, she thought, she didn't know what was happening yet, but something definitely wasn't right and Miss Browne was involved.

She thought her aunt was tidy but Miss Browne's room was immaculate. Her bed looked as if she hadn't slept in it. Libby opened the drawers carefully, making sure she didn't disturb anything. She lifted up each pile of clothes, but there was nothing underneath them.

On top of the dressing table, she spotted a

wooden box. That would be the perfect place to hide something. She opened it up, but it was empty. *How peculiar*, she thought. *What's the point of an empty box?*

As she put it back on the dressing table, Libby heard a rattle. She gently shook the box. There was definitely something in there. Maybe it had a secret compartment? Inside, the box looked completely ordinary, but when Libby looked at it more closely she spotted a small nick in the wood. She pressed down on it with her fingernail and it clicked. The base of the box slid open and something sparkled inside. For a second Libby was really excited, but then she realised it was an emerald ring: the one she'd seen Miss Browne wearing on the train. Frustrated, she closed the box and sat down on the bed.

Where could she have hidden it? Libby looked round the room. She felt something hard underneath her and pulled back the duvet. It could be Miss Browne's diary. In the bottom corner it was engraved with the initials 'O W', which Libby thought was odd. Maybe it wasn't her diary after all. She knew she should put it back. She knew she really shouldn't read anyone's diary. But what if it had something vital in it that could help her aunt?

Her hands shook as she opened the book.

Quickly flicking through, she saw most of the pages just listed places they had visited. Libby checked the day of the theft: it was blank. She wondered about the woman Miss Browne had met in the Louvre. The woman in the black-and-white coat.

There was a note scribbled on that day: 'JW' written in green ink and underlined. JW. *Who is JW?* She couldn't recall Miss Browne mentioning someone with those initials. Miss Wall's first name was Jenny but she couldn't be JW. She didn't come with them to the Louvre.

Libby sighed. She was no closer to working out what was going on. The only place she hadn't checked was the bin underneath Miss Browne's desk. If she was trying to get rid of something, that might be an obvious place to put it.

The only thing in the bin were some tiny pieces of ripped-up newspaper. Libby took them out and fitted them back together, but several pieces were missing. It looked familiar, but she couldn't think why. *Could it be the piece of newspaper Miss Browne had dropped at the train station?* She tried to read the article but there wasn't enough of the text to make sense, though it did seem to be something about a ring stolen at a school. She remembered reading something about a missing ring somewhere before. Libby racked her brain, now where did she read it?

She smiled. That was it, on the train – the article in the newspaper. If only she'd had a chance to read it more carefully at the time.

Strange that it was about another theft, though she couldn't be sure with only fragments. She wanted to take them to show Connie, but she didn't want Miss Browne to notice they were missing and realise someone had been in her room.

Libby heard a noise above her and jumped. Somebody must have come back early. She popped the diary back under Miss Browne's duvet and checked around; the room looked exactly as she'd found it, not a thing out of place. She slipped through the door. She couldn't see anyone.

'Hello, who's there?' she called, her heart racing. It was completely silent. Maybe she'd imagined the noise?

Then a large meow came from the top of the stairs leading to the attic and she heard scratching. It must be that stray cat again. 'Silly cat,' said Libby, letting out a big sigh of relief.

The meowing and scratching got louder. Libby went up and opened the attic door and the ginger-and-white cat flew past her down the stairs. She was just about to close the door again when something red caught her eye.

In the corner of the attic, she lifted a pile of boxes off a red suitcase. She recognised it. It definitely couldn't be Connie's, hers was under her bed, so it had to be Miss Browne's.

*Of course, if Miss Browne had something to hide, this would be the perfect place,* thought Libby. She was desperate to take a look inside, but was worried she'd already taken too long searching. If she was quick, it might be okay. She'd have to take a chance.

The case was stuffed full of clothes and make-up, and there were even some wigs in there – *how very strange*, she thought. She felt around underneath them, hoping to find the parcel but there was no sign of it. Just as she was about to give up, she spotted a tear in the lining. Carefully she felt inside the lining and her fingers touched something that felt like a piece of paper. She managed to slide it out of the gap. It was an empty envelope. Surely this had to be a clue.

Libby sighed. It was addressed to an Ottilie White, so nothing to do with Miss Browne after all. Disappointed, she put it back, but as she did so, she noticed there was something much bigger further down the gap in the lining. It felt cube-shaped. When she pulled it out, she was thrilled. A small white box sat in the palm of her hand. This had to be it!

Libby took a deep breath and opened it.

Inside sparkled a heart-shaped brooch with large green and red jewels.

# CHAPTER 13
## A Lady in Waiting

Libby couldn't believe her eyes: the missing brooch! Was this what the man in the street had given Miss Browne? But why would he have it, if she had stolen it? Nothing made sense. Although, surely this was the proof she needed that her aunt was innocent? It was, after all, hidden in Miss Browne's case.

She began to doubt herself. Did this really prove anything? Or would the inspector just think her aunt had hidden it here?

She heard the front door slam. Panicking, she carefully slid the box back into the lining, exactly where she found it, and hid the suitcase under the boxes.

Opening the attic door, she held her breath and listened. She could hear chattering from the floor below. Connie had promised that when they got back, she would be as loud as possible to let Libby know they were in the building, so it couldn't be her.

Tiptoeing down the stairs, she climbed back into bed and hid under the covers. She'd found more than she bargained for, but it had made her even more confused. Maybe when Connie came back, she'd know what to do. Libby yawned, the lack of sleep the night before finally catching up with her.

'Libby, wake up! I can't believe you've fallen asleep,' said Connie, shaking her.

'Uh…' Libby sat up, feeling groggy. Looking at her clock, she realised she'd been asleep for an hour. 'Miss Wall sent me to check on you. You're doing a good impression of being ill,' laughed Connie.

'Rude! I am ill,' smirked Libby.

'Well, did you find anything?'

Libby looked across to make sure the door was

 135

closed and whispered, 'You're never going to believe what I found. The missing brooch!'

Connie gasped. 'In Miss Browne's room?' she said, rather too loudly. 'So she must have stolen it!'

'Sshh, Connie, someone might hear you,' said Libby. 'I wish it was that straightforward. No, I found it in the attic.'

'The attic?' repeated Connie. 'What where you doing up there?'

Libby explained how the cat had got trapped and she'd let him out.

'The problem is we don't know who put it there.' Libby sighed. 'It could have been my aunt or Miss Browne or even someone else.'

'Why would you say that?' asked Connie. 'I thought you were sure your aunt was innocent.'

'Er, well…' Libby paused. She still didn't want to tell Connie that she'd found her jewellery box in her aunt's room. 'What kind of detective would I be if I didn't consider all the different possibilities?'

'We have to tell the police,' insisted Connie. 'If we don't tell them and they find out, then we'll get in trouble.'

'No, we can't,' pleaded Libby. 'The police already suspect that my aunt stole it. I don't know why, but they have some evidence that makes her look guilty. If they find it here, they'll arrest her again.'

Connie sighed, 'I don't know, Libby. We can't just pretend it's not here.'

Libby panicked. She needed to find a way to get Connie onside. 'If she goes to prison, what will happen to us? Miss Browne could be the new head; my aunt has already put her in charge. I'll have nowhere to go and maybe you'll have to go back to that school you hated.'

'I'm definitely not going back there!' Connie paused. 'Okay, but we can't leave it up there forever.'

A knock at the door startled them. Miss Browne popped her head round. Libby glanced guiltily at Connie. *What if she had heard their conversation?*

'Are you feeling better, Libby?' asked Miss Browne, watching Libby's expression carefully. 'You look flushed. Have you got a temperature?'

Libby could feel her face getting redder and redder.

'I'm a bit hot. Maybe I'll get up for a bit.'

Downstairs, Libby tried her hardest to remember she was supposed to be ill, but the smell of the fresh bread was too much. She cut herself a large slice and spread it thickly with butter and some generous slices of *jambon*.

'I see you're feeling much better.' Miss Mousedale smiled, walking into the room. She looked at Libby closely over her glasses. 'I hope you got plenty of rest when everyone was out.'

Libby suspected her aunt knew she wasn't really ill. She'd be furious if she discovered what she'd really been doing. 'I've been fast asleep the whole time.'

'I bet she's faking it,' said Noah. 'She looks fine to me.'

Sebastian sniggered.

'That's enough, thank you, boys,' said Miss Mousedale.

Libby glared at them and turned to Connie. 'Let's go to the library, after lunch.' She said it loudly enough for everyone to hear.

'Why?' asked Connie. 'I thought we were going

to the park.'

'Because we need to finish our project. Remember!' She winked, hoping Connie would work out what she meant. She whispered, 'I thought Lady Constance might like an outing...'

'Oh, yes!' said Connie, taking the hint. 'We really must go to the library.'

'The library! Are you sure?' said Miss Mousedale. She lowered her voice. 'I hope you're not up to anything.'

'No,' said Libby innocently. 'We've got to finish our project. I've been a bit distracted recently.' She felt bad about lying to her aunt, but there was no way they'd be allowed to go to Montmartre by themselves.

'If you must. Don't forget, it's due next week,' Miss Mousedale reminded them. 'And do be sensible, Libby.'

'I'll be on my best behaviour,' she promised, her fingers crossed behind her back.

Connie went to make a phone call and Libby headed upstairs to get changed. She wished Connie would hurry up!

'All sorted,' said Connie. 'I've got Stewart to ring the shop and make an appointment, so they'll be expecting us.'

'Who's Stewart?'

'Our butler. And yes, I know most people don't have a butler.' Connie rolled her eyes. 'Please don't make a big deal of it!'

'Okay, calm down,' said Libby. She looked at Connie and grimaced. How could she say this nicely? 'The problem is you're not looking a lot like I'd expect a lady to look.'

Connie's hair was in its usual wild state and she'd somehow managed to get butter on her cheek. She looked in the mirror and horror spread across her face. 'Give me five minutes.' She rushed off to the bathroom.

Ten minutes later Connie – or Lady Constance Montgomery, as she was going to be for the new few hours – reappeared. Libby barely recognised her. Gone was the untamed hair and in its place was a sleek, impossibly smart, twisted 'up-do'. Around her neck she wore her string of pearls, and tiny pearl earrings finished off the look. She was wearing a sensible cardigan and a checked skirt. Libby tried not to laugh but couldn't help it.

'Don't you dare say anything,' warned Connie. 'I look just like my mother.'

Libby did a mock curtsey. 'Yes, Lady Constance, as you wish.'

Connie's face looked as if she was trying to be cross, but she couldn't hide her smile.

'Come on, Libby, we've got a mystery to solve.'

# Chapter 14
## A Familiar Face

Connie climbed the steps to 'Bijoutiers Deco' and rang the doorbell. There was no answer.

'Try again,' nagged Libby, hopping up and down the steps.

'It's not very polite to keep ringing the bell.'

'Who are you and what have you done with Connie?' said Libby, trying to keep her face straight.

They both looked at each other and burst into laughter.

'*Bonjour. Avez-vous un rendez-vous?*' came a voice out of thin air.

Libby nudged Connie. 'Go on. She wants to know

if you have an appointment.'

'I know,' said Connie. She tried to stop her giggles and coughed. '*Oui, au nom de Lady Constance Montgomery.* I believe my butler has phoned ahead.'

Libby stared wide-eyed at Connie, wondering where this fancy voice had come from. Connie was full of surprises.

'What?' Connie covered the speaker. 'Mother insists I speak properly when we have guests. I knew it would come in useful one day.'

'*Pardonnez-moi, Lady Constance. Entrez.*'

The door buzzed, letting them inside.

'Let me do the talking,' said Connie. 'You'll just ask too many questions.'

The *vendeuse* tried her best not to look surprised when she realised Lady Constance was a schoolgirl, but Libby could see the confusion in her eyes.

'How can I be of assistance?'

Connie smiled her most charming smile. 'I've been sent by my father to find a piece of jewellery for my mother.' She looked around at the displays. 'I do believe he requires a brooch, the more jewels the better. It's for a special birthday.'

'Well, we did have rather an exceptional art deco brooch,' she sighed. 'But unfortunately…'

'Yes, we heard all about that, must have been terrible for you.' Connie sighed sympathetically. 'Such a shame, I'm sure that would have been perfect.'

'We do have some other smaller brooches I would be pleased to show you.'

'How marvellous,' said Connie.

Libby had to dig her fingernails into her hand to stop herself giggling. It was so strange seeing Connie like this.

The *vendeuse* carefully unlocked the glass cabinet and retrieved a velvet cushion with the most stunning brooches displayed on it. They looked tiny compared to the missing brooch, but Libby couldn't help being dazzled.

'Oooh, they're all so pretty,' she gasped.

Connie glared at Libby. 'Apologies for my companion, she's not used to the finer things in life.'

Libby glared back. She wasn't

sure she liked this new bossy version of her friend.

Connie looked at each of the brooches closely, as if she was actually considering buying one, asking questions about the cut and clarity of the jewels. Libby had no idea what she was talking about, but it all sounded very convincing.

'Must have been awful for you,' said Connie. 'Did the thief threaten you?'

'It didn't exactly happen like that.' The *vendeuse* hesitated and looked around. 'Although I shouldn't really talk about it…'

Connie smiled. 'Of course, I completely understand. Now this is charming. It might be just the thing Father is looking for.' She picked up a brooch in the shape of a thistle. 'You were saying there were two ladies here when it happened.'

'Well, I never actually said that.' The woman looked confused.

Libby glared at Connie. She'd warned her about asking too many questions and now she was doing just that.

'Lady Constance,' Libby interrupted. 'You

remember, you read about that in the newspaper.'

'Ah, yes, that was it. Were they working together, do you think?'

Libby had to stop herself rolling her eyes. Connie was practically giving them away. She was being far too nosy.

The doorbell rang. The *vendeuse* looked at Connie nervously and then popped the cushion back into the glass case and locked it. 'One moment.' She went over to the door, pressed a button and spoke into the intercom.

'Connie, you're not exactly being subtle,' warned Libby.

'But if we don't find anything out, it's going to be a wasted trip,' said Connie.

Libby started as a tall lady wearing a blue hat with a peacock feather and a black-and-white coat entered the shop. A tall lady Libby had definitely seen before. She looked equally surprised to see them.

'*Pardonnez-moi*, I didn't realise you had customers. I will come back later,' she said, turning to go.

'Oh, please don't leave on our account,' said Libby,

imitating Connie's posh voice. 'I think Connie – I mean Lady Constance – has a lot of ideas to share with her father. I'm sure we'll be back soon.'

Connie looked surprised but said, 'Ah, yes, I have lots of rather splendid ideas. *Merci, madame.*'

Smiling at both women, Libby steered Connie out of the door and briskly down the street.

'What was all that about?' asked Connie. 'I was just getting somewhere.'

Libby grinned. 'I recognised the woman who came in the shop and I think she recognised me. She was the one Miss Browne was arguing with in the Louvre.'

'Really?' gasped Connie. 'Why was she at the jeweller's?'

'That's not all,' said Libby. 'I've seen someone outside the house *and* in the library wearing that black-and-white coat. The pattern is so distinctive it stuck in my mind.'

'So you're saying the same person who met Miss Browne has also been following us?' asked Connie.

'Yes!' said Libby.

'Why?' asked Connie.

'I don't know. Somehow she's mixed up in this,' said Libby. 'She has to be connected to Miss Browne.'

'My, my, girls, you've been very busy,' said a voice behind them. 'What have you got yourselves mixed up in?'

Libby and Connie turned round in shock. They couldn't believe their eyes. Right there in front of them stood the lady in the peacock hat!

# CHAPTER 15
## A Plan is Formed

'Returning to the scene of the crime?' she asked.

She glared at them. Libby was lost for words, transfixed by the woman's piercing blue eyes. She hadn't even heard her footsteps.

'Who are you and why are you following us?' asked Connie.

Libby was shocked. It was unlike Connie to be so bold.

She tried to pull herself together. 'You were the one talking to Miss Browne in the Louvre? Perhaps it's you that's returning to the scene!'

The woman retrieved a card from her pocket and

handed it over. 'You're quite observant. Libby, isn't it?'

Embossed in purple swirly writing, the card said:

Jocelyn Whittle
Private Investigator

Shaken, Libby passed it to Connie.

'So you're JW,' Libby said, remembering Miss Browne's diary. 'Why are you following us? Are you working with Miss Browne?'

'So many questions,' said Jocelyn. 'You really shouldn't jump to conclusions.'

Libby flushed. She was getting fed up of being told this.

'You're avoiding the question,' said Connie. 'I think you'd better tell us exactly what's going on.'

Jocelyn raised her eyebrows. *She was clearly unused to being challenged, especially by children,* thought Libby.

'You've done a really good job of getting yourselves caught up in this mess,' she said. 'But I suppose you're right. I do owe you an explanation.' She pointed to the café across the road. 'Maybe we need to talk somewhere a bit quieter?'

'Okay,' said Libby.

'Libby,' said Connie, grabbing her arm and pulling her to one side. 'We don't know anything about this woman and you want to go and have a cosy chat with her?'

'What could go wrong?' insisted Libby. 'The café is a public place. Everyone can see us. I really need to find out what's going on. Please, Connie!'

'I promise you can trust me,' said Jocelyn.

Connie looked at her suspiciously. 'You would say that.' She paused. 'Fine, we'll come, but you've got ten minutes.'

In the café, Libby ordered herself a large pastry. She took a huge bite as Jocelyn started to talk.

'I'm not sure how much you know, but somehow you and your aunt have been implicated in this theft.'

'Me?' Libby spluttered crumbs everywhere.

'Yes. You caused the distraction while your aunt was in the jeweller's,' said Jocelyn.

'But...' It was the first time anyone had confirmed

her fear, that somehow she'd let this happen.

'I know it looks bad for you and your aunt, Libby, but I don't actually think you're involved,' said Jocelyn.

'Why do you think my aunt is innocent?' It was what she wanted to hear, but something nagged at the back of her mind. There was still the mystery of why Connie's jewellery box was in her aunt's room.

'How do we know you're not involved and this isn't some kind of trick?' asked Connie.

Jocelyn looked annoyed. 'You have to believe me.'

'Why?' asked Connie defiantly. 'You could be anyone, for all we know.'

Libby leaped in. 'You clearly know Miss Browne. Maybe you planned it together. I remember now. I saw you on the train. You were looking for someone.'

Jocelyn shook her head. 'You're right, I was looking for Miss Browne.' She paused. 'I'm impressed by your observational skills. Maybe I should recruit you when you're older.'

'I'm not waiting till I'm older,' said Libby. 'My aunt has been accused of a crime she hasn't committed. It's up to me to prove she's innocent.'

'Okay, I understand that.' Jocelyn sighed. 'I think I need to start at the beginning. Miss Browne isn't who she claims to be. Her real name is Ottilie White.'

'Ottilie White? I recognise that name. It was on a letter hidden in Miss Browne's case,' she said. 'Did you send the letter?'

'I wrote to her giving her a final chance to return the ring. The owners don't want to make a fuss. They just want their ring back.'

Jocelyn explained that she had first met Miss Browne when the teacher was accused of stealing a ring last year. Despite her investigations and Miss Browne's obvious guilt, she had never been able to prove she was involved.

'When I discovered she was moving to Paris, I followed her here,' said Jocelyn. 'She obviously changed her identity and now she's stolen again but this time she's got your aunt involved.'

'So that's why you've been hanging around,' said Libby.

'I was hoping she'd slip up and I could catch her red-handed,' said Jocelyn. 'But she's far too clever and now something else has gone missing. It's too much of a coincidence.'

'What did the ring look like?' Libby asked.

Jocelyn looked confused. 'If you must know, it was gold with a large emerald in the middle. Very distinctive.'

'I saw her wearing a big green ring the first time I saw her on the train, but when she got off at the station it had disappeared.'

'She must have sold it then. But, I've been following her everywhere. How could I have missed it?'

Libby blushed. 'I might have found it in her room. It was hidden in a box on her dressing table.'

'What were you doing in her room?' asked Jocelyn. 'You really are quite the inquisitive girl.'

'I knew my aunt was innocent. I had to do something!' Libby breathed a sigh of relief. She felt terrible for ever doubting her aunt.

'So Miss Browne, or whatever she's really called, is a thief,' said Connie. 'You were right all along, Libby.'

'How do we prove it?'

Jocelyn sighed. 'I don't know. If we could only find

a way to link her to the brooch, but she's probably sold it on by now.'

'There's one thing I haven't mentioned,' Libby admitted. 'I also found the missing brooch at school.'

'What? How? Why haven't you informed the inspector?' asked Jocelyn, clearly shocked.

'Why didn't you tell the police about Miss Browne's past when that brooch was stolen?' replied Libby. 'Then my aunt would never have been arrested!'

Jocelyn shrugged. 'I had no proof, but you have – you have the brooch. Tell the *gendarmes* and then your aunt will be in the clear.'

Libby blushed. 'Either my aunt or Miss Browne could have hidden it in the attic, and I couldn't be sure my aunt was innocent after I found Connie's jewellery box in her room.'

'You never told me that!' said Connie. 'Why would she have my jewellery box?'

'I'm sorry, I didn't want you to think she was capable of stealing from you,' said Libby. 'It's definitely yours – it has a thistle engraved on the top.'

'But mine hasn't got a thistle on it,' said Connie.

'My locket has a thistle.'

Libby went even redder. How could she have got it so wrong?

'Girls, I'm completely lost,' interrupted Jocelyn. 'Are you sure you're not mistaken, Libby? How do you know you've found the right brooch?'

'It's definitely the one. We saw a picture in the newspaper of the missing brooch, and it's really unusual.'

Jocelyn thought for a moment. 'There is one way we could find out who is really involved.' She smiled. 'And you did say you wanted to clear your aunt's name.'

'Okay,' said Libby, knowing she would do anything for her aunt. 'What can I do?'

'Libby,' Connie warned. 'Be careful. This isn't…'

'I know, it isn't one of my mystery stories,' said Libby. 'But if it helps Aunt Agatha, I have to try!'

'Don't worry, I don't have anything dangerous in mind. I promise,' said Jocelyn.

'Wait.' Connie stared at Libby firmly. 'We're not agreeing to anything until we hear the plan.'

'Okay,' said Libby. She couldn't really think straight.

She wasn't going to give up this chance to clear her aunt, despite anything Connie might say.

Jocelyn said, 'Here's what we're going to do.'

# CHAPTER 16
## A Night at the Opera

'Girls, where have you been?' asked Miss Mousedale. 'You need to get ready – we're leaving in half an hour.'

Libby was confused. Her aunt hadn't said anything about going out this evening. She wanted time to work out how to put Jocelyn's plan into action.

'How lovely,' said Connie, sweetly. 'Where are we going?'

Miss Mousedale beamed. 'Miss Browne has kindly treated us to tickets at the opera. I've always wanted to go to the Opéra Garnier and it's my favourite, *La Bohème*.'

Libby frowned when she heard Miss Browne's name. But she remembered she had to be careful. She couldn't afford to let her aunt know her true feelings, not until they found some proof. 'Isn't Miss Browne kind!'

'Such a shame I can't join you,' said Miss Browne, appearing at the door. 'Unfortunately they didn't have enough tickets.'

'You can go instead of me,' said Noah. 'It sounds really boring.'

'I obviously can't trust you to be here by yourself, Noah,' said Miss Mousedale. 'Anyway, I rang the ticket office and they had a last-minute cancellation, so you can come after all, Louisa.'

Libby saw Miss Browne turn pale. 'I don't have time to change,' she said. 'I'll make you late.'

'Nonsense,' said Miss Mousedale. 'Libby and Connie still have to get ready. We have plenty of time.'

Libby forced herself to smile. Miss Browne mustn't realise they knew just what kind of person she was.

'You must come,' said Libby. 'It won't be the same without you.'

Upstairs, Libby searched through her wardrobe trying to find something suitable. 'I've got nothing to wear. Are jeans okay?'

'Hang on, my mum's packed loads of smart clothes. I haven't even worn most of them,' said Connie. She rifled through her suitcase.

Libby doubted anything of Connie's would fit her, but she supposed it was better than wearing her tatty jeans. Her aunt looked happier than she had in ages and she didn't want to annoy her by looking a mess.

'If everyone is out, this will be the perfect time for Jocelyn to come over and set everything up. I'll text her,' said Libby, taking out her phone.

'Here you go,' said Connie, throwing a velvet top at her. 'I think that's long enough to be a dress on you.'

Libby struggled to get into it. 'I look ridiculous.'

Connie laughed. 'Stop moaning or I'll make you wear the pearls as well!'

\*\*\*

As Libby followed the rest of the pupils on to the street and closed the front door,

she spotted Jocelyn waiting outside the restaurant opposite. Time to put their plan into action!

'Oh, I forgot my phone,' said Libby. 'Mum said she'd message tonight.'

'Hurry up, or we'll be late,' said Miss Mousedale.

'Can I borrow your key?'

Miss Mousedale checked her bag. 'I must have left it on my dressing table. I'm sure Miss Browne will let you borrow hers.'

'You can't,' said Miss Browne. 'I mean, I lost it weeks ago. I must have misplaced it in my room.'

'Never mind, I'll just get Monsieur Joliffe to let me in,' said Libby. 'Don't wait for me. I'll catch you up.' She rang the front doorbell and the concierge answered.

'Thank you,' she said, hurrying in.

Libby looked around to double check everyone had gone. She needed to create a distraction to get the concierge away from his desk. And she knew just the thing!

'Monsieur Joliffe,' she shouted. 'I think that cat has got in again. I can hear it scratching upstairs.'

'*Zut alors*,' he muttered and went to look for it.

Libby smiled. That was easy enough. She ran to
the door, signalled to Jocelyn and let her into the
building.

'Wait in my room till the coast is clear,' said Libby. 'It's the first one at the top of the stairs on the left.'

'Thanks, Libby. You're definitely sure no one else is in here?'

'Yes, I'm sure. I need to go. They'll be wondering where I am.'

Libby dashed down the street and was out of breath by the time she caught up with the others at the entrance to the métro.

\*\*\*

It was past midnight when they got back to school. Libby was exhausted. It had been a really long and stressful day.

'Right, brush your teeth and straight to bed,' ordered Miss Mousedale.

Libby hoped Jocelyn had managed to set everything up in time. Now all she had to do was wait and keep her fingers crossed their plan would work.

'I can't believe you thought your aunt had taken my jewellery box,' said Connie, as they climbed into bed.

'Don't remind me. I feel awful about it,' said Libby. 'I wonder what happened to it?'

'No idea. Luckily it's not valuable or I'd be in big trouble.'

'I know Jocelyn said we shouldn't go near it,' said Libby. 'But should we sneak up and look at the brooch tomorrow?'

'I don't know…' said Connie. 'What if someone catches us with it? How will we explain?'

'We'll just need to be careful.' Libby leaned over to turn off her bedside light. 'You worry too much.'

The next morning the girls sat silently eating their breakfast. Libby was too nervous to say anything, just in case she gave the game away. She barely touched her croissant.

'You're unusually quiet,' said Miss Mousedale.

Libby tried to change the subject. 'I was just thinking I hadn't heard from Mum in ages. I really hope she's back for Christmas.' She felt bad for lying but she couldn't tell her aunt the truth.

'I hope so too,' said Miss Mousedale. 'I've hardly seen her since … well, it feels like a long time.'

Libby knew what she meant. Since her dad had gone, they hadn't stayed in one place long enough to spend time with anyone.

'Let's look at our *project* after breakfast,' said Connie.

'Project? What project?' Libby realised what Connie meant. 'Oh, *that* project! Yes! We need to finish it.'

'Girls, have you still not finished your work?' asked Miss Mousedale. 'Connie, I was hoping you'd be a good influence on Libby.'

Libby smirked. 'Yeah, you're such a bad influence Connie.' She winked at her friend.

Some of the other students, including Noah and Sebastian, had gone to the shops with Miss Wall and Miss Browne. Libby was glad they'd said they were going to finish their schoolwork. It gave them the perfect excuse to stay behind. Miss Mousedale was working in her study. They checked that no one else was around and crept up to the attic.

'Where's it hidden?' asked Connie, looking round the room.

'It's over there in the suitcase,' said Libby. 'We need to be careful. We can't disturb anything.'

Libby slowly slid the suitcase out and lifted the lid. She searched inside the lining but it wasn't there. Where could it be? She emptied out the entire contents of the suitcase. But there was no white box anywhere.

'Connie, the brooch…' she stuttered. 'It's gone!'

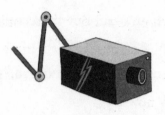

# CHAPTER 17
### The Truth at Last

Libby rang Jocelyn and arranged to meet her at the café opposite the library. They needed to tell her about the missing brooch as soon as possible. Connie knocked on Miss Mousedale's door to let her know they were leaving. 'We're off to the library.'

'Again?' asked Miss Mousedale. 'Okay, but make sure you're back by lunch. We've got grammar practice planned for this afternoon.'

Connie tried to smile. 'Sounds like fun.'

As they hurried to the café, Connie asked, 'Libby, you don't think Jocelyn could have taken the brooch, do you? It disappeared after we let her into the school.'

'You're thinking like a detective at last!' said Libby, delighted. 'But if she had stolen the brooch, she wouldn't be arranging to meet with us, she'd have disappeared by now!'

'Good point,' said Connie.

Jocelyn was already there waiting for them. Libby explained that the brooch had disappeared. 'Maybe I imagined seeing it,' she said, doubting herself.

'I think that's unlikely. You're far too observant. Time to find out exactly what's been going on.' Jocelyn opened up three different screens on her laptop and turned it round so that Libby and Connie could see.

'So this is the camera feed for last night,' said Jocelyn. 'And this one is this morning, right up until when you phoned me. Let me just speed it up a bit. Watch carefully for anyone or anything unusual.'

Libby and Connie stared at the screen, desperate to see something that might help. There were lots of images of Monsieur Joliffe searching for the cat, but nothing interesting.

'Somebody must have taken it before you put the

cameras there,' groaned Libby. 'This isn't going to help.'

'Look, someone's there!' said Connie.

A shadow appeared coming down the stairs from the attic. It quickly crossed the landing and went down the stairs.

'They must have the brooch,' said Libby. 'Where have they gone now?'

'Let me just check the other cameras,' said Jocelyn.

The mysterious person walked into the shot in front of the door to Miss Mousedale's room, but they had their back to the camera, so the girls couldn't see their face. The bedroom door opened and they disappeared inside.

'Quickly, change cameras,' said Libby impatiently.

Jocelyn clicked on the screen and zoomed in on the figure inside Miss Mousedale's room.

'Well, that's definitely not Miss Browne. It's a man,' said Connie.

'And if you look at the time,' said Libby. 'She has the perfect alibi. We were all out together at the opera for the evening.'

'But don't you remember? Miss Browne wasn't

meant to be going to the opera. Maybe she had to change her plans and that's why he's here,' said Connie.

The man had something in his hand. They could see him hovering over Miss Mousedale's bed. After a few minutes, he turned round and his face was captured clearly by the camera as he left the room.

'Wait,' said Libby. Something was familiar about him. 'Go back. Can you freeze that image of his face?'

Jocelyn moved the film back until she found him and pressed pause. Libby stared closely at him.

'Look, he's wearing a bow tie. I'm sure I've seen him before!'

Jocelyn said, 'Do you know who he is?'

Libby checked in her bag for her camera. 'I don't.' She scrolled through her images. She'd taken so many since they arrived in Paris. 'But I'm sure it's the same man I saw arguing with Miss Browne.'

'The man on the bridge?' asked Connie. 'Let's hope you haven't deleted it.'

'Found it,' Libby said triumphantly. She zoomed in on the picture so they could all see his face more clearly, and held it next to the laptop.

'Libby, that's brilliant,' said Jocelyn. 'It definitely looks like the same man. We need to work out who he is and why he was in the school.'

'And we need to find out how he's connected to Miss Browne,' said Libby.

'We need to do it quickly,' said Connie. 'What if this man has planted the brooch in your aunt's room?'

'Why do you say that?' asked Libby.

'It's the only thing that makes sense,' said Connie. 'Miss Browne arranged for us all to be out. She seems determined to frame your aunt.'

'Maybe she's planning to tip the *gendarmes* off. If they find the brooch, your aunt will be rearrested and charged with theft,' said Jocelyn.

'And then Miss Browne will be in charge of the school,' sighed Connie.

'Won't this video prove she's not guilty?' asked Libby. She couldn't believe they'd gone to all this trouble and Miss Browne had outwitted them.

Jocelyn grimaced. 'It would be if we could show anyone. But technically we've filmed this illegally so it can't be used as evidence.' She paused. 'We need to find another way to catch Miss Browne in the act.'

'What if we retrieve the brooch and put it in her room?' suggested Libby.

'Libby,' said Connie, horrified. 'You can't do that.'

'Why not? It seems fair enough to me,' said Libby stubbornly.

'I have to agree with Connie. Not only is it highly unethical, if we get caught then we will all be implicated,' said Jocelyn.

Libby thought hard. There must be a way to catch Miss Browne. She smiled. 'I've got an idea! We need to play Miss Browne at her own game.'

'Go on, I'm listening,' said Jocelyn.

Libby outlined her plan to Jocelyn and Connie. 'I know it's a risk but I don't know what else we can do.'

'That just might work,' agreed Jocelyn. 'Let's hope she falls for it!'

'I really hope so,' said Libby, sighing. She was beginning to feel desperate. 'This might be our last chance.'

# Chapter 18
## Hook, Line and Sinker

Back in school, later that day, Libby and Connie sat nervously in class. Miss Mousedale was trying to teach them verbs and Libby could see Noah nodding off in the corner. A knock came at the door, waking him up, and the concierge came in.

'*Excusez-moi*, Mademoiselle Mousedale, I have a note for you,' said Monsieur Joliffe.

Miss Mousedale sighed. 'Can't it wait? I'm in the middle of teaching.'

'*Non, Mademoiselle.* Apparently, it is very urgent,' he said.

The noise level started creeping up as everyone

took full advantage of the distraction.

'Silence,' said Miss Mousedale firmly. 'Please read the next page. I will be testing you in five minutes.'

A groan went round the room. Libby watched her aunt anxiously, trying to gauge her reaction. Miss Mousedale stared intently at the note and then her eyes filled with tears. Sitting down on her chair, she let out a huge sigh of relief.

'I'm saved,' she said.

Libby tried not to smile. It looked like the plan was working. 'Miss Mousedale, have you had some good news?'

'Yes! I've had a letter from Inspecteur de Villiers. Apparently the brooch has turned up and the owners are not going to press any charges.'

Libby did her best to look surprised. 'Really? That's fab!'

She felt guilty for deceiving her aunt but hoped she would be forgiven if it all worked out.

Miss Mousedale clapped her hands. 'Everyone, I've decided that this afternoon, instead of a test, we will go out for a treat!'

The room erupted into loud cheers. Noah in particular was extremely vocal, but for once Libby didn't mind – the noisier the better.

The door opened and Miss Browne came in. 'Miss Mousedale, is everything all right? I could hear the shouting all the way from my room.'

'Miss Browne, you'll never believe it.' She smiled. 'The brooch has been found and handed in. So the case has been dropped.'

'Er, that's wonderful,' stuttered Miss Browne.

'You don't have to worry about being in charge anymore,' said Miss Mousedale. 'Isn't that wonderful?'

Miss Mousedale was too happy to notice that Miss Browne wasn't at all pleased. She looked very alarmed. Libby was watching her and saw the flash of panic in her eyes. She couldn't help feeling satisfaction at unnerving Miss Browne. Fingers crossed, the teacher would try to retrieve the brooch and then they would have their proof.

'We must celebrate. My treat,' said Miss Mousedale. 'Are you coming?'

Miss Browne rubbed her head. 'I'm sorry, I feel like I'm getting a migraine. I don't want to spoil your fun.'

'Oh no, you poor thing, you must go and lie down,' said Miss Mousedale sympathetically. 'I'll bring you something back from the patisserie. Hopefully you'll feel better later.'

Libby smiled at Connie. Their plan was working!

Miss Mousedale took them all to their favourite patisserie. Although it was cold, they sat outside under the heaters, enjoying the most gorgeous pastries and cakes. There was a real buzz in the air. Everyone was chattering away. Sebastian was trying to see how many macarons he could fit in his mouth at once. Libby could see how happy her aunt was, but she still felt terrible. What if their plan didn't work?

'Are you okay?' Miss Mousedale asked her. 'You look as if you're in a world of your own.'

Libby hated to lie to her aunt but she couldn't tell her the truth. 'I was just thinking about my mum and how she'd love to be here with us.'

'Have you heard from her lately? I haven't had a letter in weeks.'

'I've had this from her this morning.' Libby took a postcard out of her bag.

'She says she's on her way to Peru.'

'Peru?' said Miss Mousedale. 'That's strange, she didn't mention it in her last letter.' She took the postcard from Libby.

'I know.' Libby wasn't sure why her aunt looked so concerned. 'She's had a lead on a new job and she couldn't turn it down.' Libby was worried that this new job might mean her mum wouldn't be home for Christmas. Maybe that was her aunt's concern as well.

'I can't help wondering who had the brooch all this time,' said Miss Mousedale. 'Maybe I should drop by the police station later. I need to collect my passport anyway.'

Libby sat up, alarmed. 'Er, I wouldn't do that.'

'Why ever not?' said Miss Mousedale. 'Are you all right? You look rather pale.'

'It's just…' Libby tried to think of something, anything, to put her aunt off going to the police station.

'I think what Libby is trying to say,' said Connie, 'is you need to enjoy today. You can collect your passport tomorrow.'

'Shall I get some macarons to take home for Miss

Browne?' asked Libby, to distract her aunt.

'Oh, well remembered. Yes, a box of twelve,' said Miss Mousedale. She handed her a one hundred euro note. 'That should cover the bill for everything, hopefully.'

'Connie, help me choose,' said Libby, gesturing for her to come to the counter. 'Phew, that was close. Have you heard from Jocelyn yet?'

Connie checked her phone. 'Not yet. She said she'd message as soon as she knew Miss Browne had the brooch.'

The minutes seemed to drag by and still there was no message from Jocelyn. Libby kept checking her watch, anxious for news.

'I think it's time to get back to school,' said Miss Mousedale.

Libby panicked. 'No, not yet!'

'Why ever not?' asked Miss Mousedale. 'You can't still be hungry.'

'I'm still finishing my hot chocolate,' said Libby. She took a small sip, determined to make it last as long as she needed, even though it had gone cold.

Just as Libby thought she was going to burst, Connie signalled to her to come over.

'It's brilliant news. Miss Browne has done exactly as we hoped: she's taken the brooch from Miss Mousedale's room,' whispered Connie with a huge grin across her face. 'Jocelyn is going to ring Inspecteur de Villiers now and leave a tip-off.'

'I'm all finished. Let's go,' Libby declared with relief, pretending to finish her drink. 'It must be nearly dinner, I'm starving.'

Miss Mousedale laughed. 'Make your mind up.' She looked at her watch. 'We had better go back. Madame Roux will be really cross if we're late for dinner.'

They headed back to school. Miss Mousedale was so happy, even Noah clowning around didn't seem to bother her. Instead of shouting at him, she just laughed. 'Noah, please be careful. I don't want you to break your other arm.'

As they turned the corner onto their street, Miss Mousedale stopped, looking shocked. Outside the school was a police car and Inspecteur de Villiers was waiting by the front door.

# CHAPTER 19
## An Unexpected Visitor

'But, I don't understand,' said Miss Mousedale. 'I got your message this morning.' She opened up her desk and took out the note which she handed to Inspecteur de Villiers.

The inspector looked at the note closely, clearly puzzled. 'I did not send this. This is a falsehood. Clearly someone has played a cruel trick on you, Mademoiselle Mousedale. This is not from me,' he said indignantly.

Libby tried not to catch her aunt's eye. She knew

her aunt would be furious if she found out what she'd done.

'We need to speak to Mademoiselle Browne. We have had an anonymous tip off that she may be able to help us with our enquiries,' said the inspector.

'Are you now trying to say she's involved?' asked Miss Mousedale. 'First me, now her. Whatever is going on?'

'I cannot go into details but I must speak to her at once.'

'But of course,' said Miss Mousedale politely. 'She's in bed with a migraine.'

Miss Mousedale went upstairs. A moment later, she reappeared. 'She's not there.'

'This is ridiculous,' said the inspector. 'I must see for myself.'

He stormed up the stairs, with Libby and Connie closely behind.

Miss Mousedale shouted, 'You can see for yourself she's not here. I can assure you, I have nothing to hide.'

'The attic,' said Libby and Connie at the same time.

'What?' asked the inspector.

'Miss Browne has been storing her things in the attic. She might be hiding up there,' said Libby. She dashed past the inspector and headed up the narrow stairs.

'Libby, wait,' called Connie, following hot on her heels.

The inspector stared after them. '*Gendarmes*,' he instructed. 'Follow those girls.'

'Libby? Connie? What on earth is going on?' shouted Miss Mousedale. She stood at the bottom of the stairs in complete shock.

Libby pushed open the attic door. The room was empty and there was no sign of Miss Browne.

'Look! The window is open,' said Connie.

They both rushed over. Libby leaned outside. She could see Miss Browne climbing her way down the drainpipe.

'I'm going after her,' said Libby. 'She's not getting away with it this time!'

'Don't, it's too dangerous,' warned Connie. 'We don't know what she's capable of.'

Libby ignored Connie and swung her leg over

the window ledge. She tried to feel for the drainpipe but it was just out of reach. Miss Browne obviously had longer arms than her.

The *gendarmes* burst into the room. Libby looked at the distance to the drainpipe. *It's not that far*, she told herself and stretched, grabbing some ivy on the wall to steady herself. She scraped her knee on the wall as she clambered on to the drainpipe. Ignoring the pain, she slowly shimmied down, placing her foot on the windowsill to steady herself. Libby's heart was racing but she didn't have time to be scared, she could see Miss Browne had made it down to the ground.

Miss Browne must have heard something because she looked up. 'Libby, stay out of this,' she warned.

Libby scrambled down as quickly as she dared. She could feel the drainpipe was starting to move away from the wall.

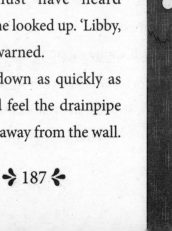

Terrified, she clung on and forced herself not to look down. There was no way she was going to let her escape.

As she reached the bottom, she could see Miss Browne halfway across the courtyard at the back of the buildings. There was still no sign of the *gendarmes*. There seemed to be a commotion at the top of the building but nobody was following her down.

'Libby, be careful,' shouted Connie in the distance.

Libby felt she had no choice but to run after Miss Browne. Her knee was throbbing and she could feel blood trickling down her leg, but she gritted her teeth and carried on. She had no idea what she would do if she caught up with her. Perhaps she could stall her just until the *gendarmes* arrived.

'It's no use,' yelled Libby. 'You'll never get away. There are police surrounding the whole area,' she bluffed.

Miss Browne stopped in her tracks and turned around slowly. Libby could see she had rattled her.

'I'm warning you, Libby, don't mess with me.'

Libby's hand shook. 'I can prove you took the

brooch,' she stuttered. 'And tried to frame my aunt.'

She glared at her. 'I'm fed up of you interfering, Libby. You just can't help yourself. I bet it was you who sent that note.'

'It wasn't actually,' said Libby. She smiled. 'It was Jocelyn Whittle.'

Miss Browne's eyes flared. 'Jocelyn? I thought she'd given up.'

Libby had to keep distracting her. There was still no sign of anyone and she could see Miss Browne was desperate to get away.

'No, she's been in Paris the whole time and I know this isn't the first thing you've stolen, is it, Miss Browne? Or should that be Miss White?'

'What? How did you know?' said Miss Browne flabbergasted.

Libby smiled. 'How do I know that your real name is Ottilie White and that you've stolen before? I should have thought that was obvious.'

'Jocelyn!' snapped Miss Browne. 'You can't prove anything, you're just a child. Nobody will believe you!'

'You might as well give yourself up,' said Libby. 'If you confess, it might help.'

Behind her, Libby could see a car pulling up, blocking the exit to the alley. She knew she should leave it to the *gendarmes* now, but she was determined to discover why Miss Browne had framed her aunt, even if it meant putting herself in danger.

'Why did you do it?' she asked, taking a hesitant

step forward. 'My aunt's never done anything to hurt you.'

Miss Browne glared at Libby. 'Don't be so naïve, this has nothing to do with your aunt. It was all about the school. With your aunt out of the way, it would have been the perfect cover for me.'

Libby could hear footsteps running towards her.

'Libby,' shouted Connie. 'Are you okay?' She rushed up and hugged her.

'Well, isn't this very touching,' sneered Miss Browne. 'Sadly, it's time for me to go!'

She turned round and walked straight into the arms of a *gendarme*.

# CHAPTER 20
## Reunited

Back in the school, Libby and Connie were made to sit in the dining room and receive a very stern telling off from both Miss Mousedale and the inspector. Libby couldn't believe it. After everything they'd done!

'How could you be so silly?' asked Miss Mousedale, cleaning up Libby's knee. 'You're lucky this is the only thing that happened. It could have been far worse.'

Her knee stung. 'I'm sorry,' she mumbled, pulling a face.

'I have to agree with Mademoiselle Mousedale. This is police business, it is not for school children to get involved,' said the inspector gruffly.

Libby sighed. She had hoped they might have got some praise for helping to catch Miss Browne. Connie was bright red. Libby knew she hated being in trouble, and it was all her fault. She'd dragged her friend into this mess.

'What about the brooch?' asked Libby. 'Did you find it?'

The inspector blushed. '*Non*, we have conducted a thorough search of Mademoiselle Browne's room and it is nowhere to be found.'

'I think we may be able to help you with that,' suggested Connie. 'Er, I mean, if you'd like us to.'

'Unless you think we shouldn't get involved, as we're only schoolchildren,' said Libby.

The inspector narrowed his eyes. 'Are you telling me that my officers have missed something? You seem to know everything!'

Libby tried not to smile – she didn't want to annoy the inspector any more. He already looked furious!

Upstairs in Miss Browne's room, Libby pointed to the box on the dressing table.

'That was one of the first places we checked,

Inspecteur,' said one of the *gendarmes*.

'You see,' said the inspector, 'they have made a thorough search.'

Libby knocked on the bottom of the box and it made a hollow noise. 'I think they may have missed this.' Pressing on the corner inside the box, the base moved and slid open. Inside, just as she expected, was the missing brooch and the emerald ring. There was also something else that hadn't been there before, a letter.

The inspector blushed. 'Obviously you are very familiar with this box, young lady. Now why is that?' He looked at Libby suspiciously.

Libby knew if she told them the truth, it would give Jocelyn away. She had to think of an excuse. 'Er, I have a very similar box at home. We picked it up on our travels.' She looked at Connie for help.

'I remember you telling me about that,' said Connie quickly. 'Isn't that where you used to hide your secret stash of sweets?'

'Yes!' *We might get away with this*, thought Libby. 'I saw it in here when Miss Browne invited us in for

♣ 194 ♣

macarons and wondered if it was the same.'

She handed over the letter to the inspector. 'This was in there too. It might be a clue.'

Miss Mousedale looked puzzled and came closer to the inspector. 'Can I have a look? I recognise the address.'

'Of course,' said the inspector. 'Does it belong to you?'

'Not exactly,' said Miss Mousedale, reading the letter. 'This is to the board of trustees for the school from Miss Browne. I don't believe it! She's offering to take on the position of head.'

'When I was trying to stall Miss Browne, she said something about getting you out of the way,' said Libby. 'That your job would be the perfect cover.'

The inspector looked intrigued. 'This might be a little unconventional but maybe we should ask her. Fetch Mademoiselle Browne,' he instructed the *gendarme*.

When they brought her in, Miss Browne was handcuffed. She looked at Libby furiously, as if everything was her fault.

'Louisa, why did you do this?' asked Miss Mousedale. 'I thought we were friends.'

'If you could leave the questioning to me,' said the inspector firmly. 'Why did you want to blame Miss Mousedale?'

'Isn't it obvious?' laughed Miss Browne. 'Or are you too clueless to figure it out?'

Libby could see her aunt's eyes welling with tears. 'You wanted my job so badly, you would have let me go to jail?'

'It's not personal, Agatha. I thought being the head would be perfect for me,' said Miss Browne.

Libby frowned. She knew Miss Browne was being deliberately evasive. 'If it was all about the job, why was that other man involved?'

Miss Browne looked surprised.

Libby saw Connie slip out of the room. She had a hunch where she might be going.

'What man?' asked the inspector. He narrowed his eyes at Libby. 'So there's even more that you've not told me?'

Libby nodded. She was excited to explain what

they'd found out. 'We first thought that Miss Browne was acting strangely when we saw her arguing with a man on a bridge, when she was meant to be in bed with a migraine.'

Miss Browne's eyes flashed. 'You think you're so clever, Libby. You have no proof.'

'What do you mean?' asked Miss Mousedale. 'You knew that something was going on all of this time and you didn't say?'

'I couldn't be sure. Even Connie didn't believe me at first,' said Libby.

'Well, you do have an overactive imagination.' Connie grinned as she walked back in and handed Libby her camera.

Libby scrolled through the pictures. 'Here he is,' she said, giving the camera to the inspector.

'Well, well, well. That is a face I haven't seen in a while. Luc Cardon, renowned forger and jewel thief. So this is your partner in crime, Mademoiselle Browne?'

'I have no idea who that man is,' said Miss Browne. 'I just bumped into him in the street and he was furious because he spilled his coffee.'

'Well, if that's so,' said Libby, 'what was he doing in the school? And on the night that Connie's jewellery box went missing from her case?'

'The case that looks exactly like yours,' Connie added. 'Did he mistake our room for yours? Maybe he was looking for the ring!'

'What ring?' said Miss Mousedale and Inspecteur de Villiers in unison.

'This emerald ring,' said Libby, holding it up to show them. 'I think you'll find that's stolen too.'

'This is ridiculous,' said Miss Browne. 'Are you really going to listen to these silly schoolgirls?'

Libby didn't know for sure if she had all the pieces of the puzzle, but she was determined to uncover the truth. 'It was very clever of you to change your name so that my aunt couldn't discover the reason you left your last school.'

Miss Mousedale blushed. 'That can't be possible,' she stuttered. 'I had references from her last school.'

'I bet they're forged,' said Libby. 'There's no such person as Louisa Browne. This is Ottilie White.'

Everyone stared at her.

'How do you know all this?' asked Miss Mousedale.

Libby had to think quickly. 'When Miss Browne collected me from the train station, she dropped a newspaper clipping about the theft of the ring. I didn't make the connection at the time but things soon began to add up. If the inspector checks with the authorities in England, I'm sure they will confirm my suspicions,' said Libby.

'Libby, none of this makes sense,' said Miss Mousedale. 'Louisa didn't have time to steal the brooch, she was never by herself!'

Miss Browne sneered. 'I took the brooch before you even left the shop. Neither you or the assistant noticed it was gone until afterwards.'

'But that still doesn't explain what it has to do with me?' asked Miss Mousedale.

Libby could see her aunt was looking more and more confused.

'It's nothing to do with you, Agatha,' laughed Miss Browne, looking proud to admit the truth. 'You're so gullible, it was easy to convince you to give me a job. I thought you would be the ideal person to blame for the theft. And then I realised a travelling school would be the perfect way to help me smuggle jewels from country to country.'

'Well, I think that's the confession we've been looking for,' interrupted the inspector. 'Take her away.'

'You think you're very clever, girls, but I will get my own back, one day. Just you wait and see,' hissed Miss Browne, as the *gendarme* led her out of the room.

Miss Mousedale sat down on the bed. Her eyes were filled with tears. 'I think I owe you both an apology. If it wasn't for you, I could have lost everything.'

'I'm just sorry you got mixed up in this,' said Libby. 'You weren't to know that Miss Browne wasn't who she said she was. Why would you even suspect her?'

'Well, at least it's all cleared up,' said Connie. 'I can't believe we managed to stop her.'

'Time to celebrate,' said Libby. 'How about I make us a hot chocolate?'

Connie laughed. 'Any excuse. Lots of whipped cream and marshmallows on mine, please.'

'Girls, you always know how to make me smile,' said Miss Mousedale. 'Perhaps we can persuade Madame Roux to rustle us up some snacks. You deserve a reward after all this!'

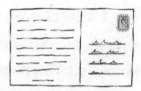

# CHAPTER 21
## End of term

The mood in the school for the next few weeks was very strange. Even though her name had been completely cleared, her aunt was very subdued. Miss Browne's betrayal was obviously still playing on her mind. In her letters to her mum, Libby hadn't dared mention what had happened. She knew she'd be furious with Libby for putting herself at risk.

Libby's mum hadn't told her what she was doing in Peru, which was unusual. Usually her mum's letters were full of details, about the people she had met, the food she had eaten and photos of her trip. She was never afraid to try out the local delicacies and over the years she had convinced Libby to try some weird and not always wonderful foods. But the last message she'd had from her mum was just a postcard, saying she was missing her and she hoped she'd be back soon. It was most unlike her.

Although they didn't have long left in Paris, Libby and Connie decided to get out the Christmas tree and decorations. Libby thought it might cheer her aunt up and she remembered seeing some boxes in the attic. They clearly hadn't been opened for years.

Libby blew off the thick layer of dust and it flew right into Connie's face. She coughed and laughed. 'Urrgghh, Libby!'

'Sorry,' she giggled, wiping dust all over her dungarees. They hauled the boxes downstairs.

'I can't believe it's only two more weeks till we leave Paris,' said Connie, sighing. She scattered some tinsel on the tree.

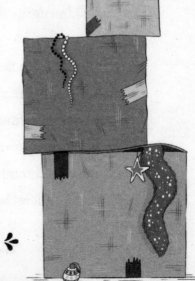

Libby smiled. 'It's definitely been an eventful term. Where shall I put this?' She held up a bright purple and red bauble.

Connie grimaced. 'Maybe at the back, where no one can see it?' she giggled.

Noah was trying to unravel the Christmas lights, and Sebastian was unhelpfully trying to wrap them round himself.

'Seb, you're making it worse,' moaned Noah. 'You're such an idiot.'

Libby laughed. It was good to see Noah getting a taste of his own medicine. 'You make quite a fetching tree, Sebastian.'

'Don't encourage him,' said Noah. 'Although, if we wrap him up in the lights, it might stop him annoying me.'

Sebastian pulled a face. Noah couldn't resist joining in and they soon both ended up in a real tangle.

'Have you heard from your mum about Christmas yet?' asked Connie. 'You could always stay at mine. I'm sure Mum wouldn't mind. We've got plenty of room.'

'Thanks, Con. But would I need to curtsey when

I see your parents?' she teased.

'Don't you dare or I won't invite you,' said Connie. 'You're so embarrassing sometimes.' She threw a felt decoration at Libby, who ducked.

'Girls,' moaned Miss Mousedale. 'Do you have to be so noisy? I'm trying to read.'

'Sorry, Miss Mousedale,' they said in unison.

'I wish my aunt would cheer up,' said Libby. 'It's almost Christmas!'

The concierge appeared with a pile of post.

Libby jumped up. 'I'll hand them out, *merci.*' She searched through them eagerly. Her face lit up when she recognised her mum's handwriting, but it was addressed to her aunt.

'Aunt Agatha, one for you,' said Libby, trying to hide her disappointment.

Miss Mousedale smiled. 'How lovely. I haven't had a letter from your mum in a while.'

Just as Libby was convinced there was nothing for her, right at the bottom of the pile, she found it. She hugged it, grinning, and then ripped it open.

'Is that from your mum?' asked Connie.

'Yes.' Libby quickly scanned it and frowned. 'Oh, no!' She looked at her aunt. 'What does your letter say?'

Miss Mousedale looked at Libby sympathetically.

'I'm sure you're disappointed, Libby. It would have been wonderful to have your mum home for Christmas, but in the current situation it isn't looking possible.'

Libby wondered what her aunt meant by 'the current situation'. Her mum hadn't gone into too many details in her letter. She checked the date on the envelope. It had been sent three weeks ago. Fingers crossed, something might have changed since then and maybe, just maybe, her mum would be home in time after all. At the start of term, she'd promised her she would be.

'I spoke to Connie's mum earlier in the week. She offered to have us both to stay for Christmas. Would you like that?' Miss Mousedale asked.

Connie threw her arms round Libby. 'Oh, do say you'll come,' she pleaded. 'It will be so much fun with you there, instead of just being stuck with my annoying brother.'

Libby had never been to Scotland. She imagined it to be wild and untamed, a bit like Connie's hair. Perhaps this was just what her aunt needed, a change of scenery and a chance to catch up with Connie's mum.

'Okay, I'd love to come,' said Libby, hugging Connie.

'Well, that's settled,' said Miss Mousedale, looking relieved. 'I'll ring and tell your mum now, Connie.'

Libby peered out of the window. The first flurries of snow had started to fall and the Christmas lights twinkled on the trees outside. She knew Christmas with Connie's family wouldn't be the same as spending time with her mum – it would be much noisier for a start – but it might be fun. It would be a nice change not to have so much excitement. Solving a mystery had turned out to be much trickier than it seemed in books.

But you never knew what the Christmas holidays might uncover.

# Acknowledgements

The fact that this book exists is testament to the support and encouragement I have received from so many wonderful people.

At the beginning of 2020, I was feeling disheartened and disappointed after numerous rejections. Luckily for me, my very own fairy godmother Amy Sparkes chose to mentor me. With her help and advice, I completely rewrote this story, giving me the confidence to send it out into the world again. I can't thank her enough for her kindness and wisdom.

To my wonderful agent, Alice Williams who believed in this book and in me. Thank you for your sage advice, calming words and endless positivity, it really means the world to me.

I feel incredibly lucky to be publishing my debut with the wonderful team at Firefly Press. To Leonie Lock, for seeing the potential in Libby and making me believe in myself. To my editor Janet Thomas, for helping this story be the very best version it could be. I'm so proud of this book and I couldn't have done it without her. To Karen Bultiauw, whose boundless cheerleading and amazing creativity is exactly what every author needs when launching a book. To Megan Farr and Amy Low for all your hard work you do behind the scenes, I really appreciate it.

To Becka Moor, for designing and illustrating my cover and book. It has completely surpassed my expectations in every way. I'm in awe of her talent and absolute love the attention to detail that she has used to bring my characters and story to life. Working with Becka has been a real dream come to true.

To my fellow 'Waffleteers', Anne Boyère and Claire Symington for keeping me company on this rollercoaster that is the writer's life.

To all the librarians, book bloggers and teachers who have read early copies of this book and shared their reviews. I know how hard you all work to share your love of reading with children and I appreciate it, it's been a real boost.

To Emma Carroll, Katherine Woodfine, Fleur Hitchcock and Clare Povey for your splendid endorsements, I feel very honoured and quite amazed by your kind words.

Behind every author there is a band of truly wonderful people who keep them going, especially when times are tough. To Lesley Parr, Perdita Cargill, Melanie Taylor-Bessent, Emma Carroll and Louie Stowell for all the pep talks, cheering on and not letting me forget to celebrate every small achievement along the way. I wouldn't have been able to do this without your help and support, thank you!

To my parent-in-laws, Helen and Alan who have always encouraged me to pursue my dreams and believed in me.

To my lovely mum and dad, who never doubted that I could achieve whatever I wanted. They have always been proud of everything I have achieved and this book is for them.

And finally to my husband Graeme, and daughters Freya and Evie. Thank you for letting me completely ignore you and lock myself away at the weekends to write. You are my life and I love you all more than you'll ever know.

And here's an exclusive sneak peek of
Libby and Connie's next adventure...

# LIBBY AND THE HIGHLAND HEIST
## JO CLARKE

# CHAPTER 1
## A Highland View

'Connie, we're nearly here!' shouted Libby. She swung down from the top bunk, landed on the floor and shook Connie to wake her up.

Annoyingly, Connie had dropped off as soon as she got into bed, but Libby had hardly slept. Connie had been right – the top bunk of a sleeper train *was* like trying to sleep on a rollercoaster.

Connie rubbed her eyes and stretched. 'What's that awful rattling noise?'

'Ssshhh,' said Libby, throwing her pillow at her. 'It's my aunt. She snores terribly. I don't think she'd like us to tell anyone though.'

Connie giggled, 'My lips are sealed.' She snuggled back down.

'Hurry up.' Libby checked her watch. 'We might have time for some breakfast before we arrive.'

'Good plan. Or my mum will insist we have a big bowl of porridge as soon as we step through the door.'

'Bleugh,' they said in unison.

They quickly got dressed and dashed down to the Club Car. Connie persuaded the attendant to make them two bacon rolls, while Libby gazed out at the grey skies. Everything seemed so empty compared to the streets of Paris. All she could see were mountains and rivers glistening in the distance. She felt really far from home.

'Here you go.' Connie handed her a roll, distracting her.

Libby munched on hers while Connie chattered away. 'I can't wait for you to meet Bertie and James.'

'I thought you only had one brother?'

'Very funny,' laughed Connie. 'They're my dogs, silly, I've missed them so much. Unlike my brother, who is really annoying!'

Libby wondered what it was like to have a brother. Being an only child, she was used to having her mum all to herself.

'Ohhh, I think we're coming into the station now!' said Connie. 'Let's grab our bags. I know Dad will be waiting for us. He's always early.'

Connie clambered off and dashed along the platform with Libby's aunt, Miss Mousedale, in close pursuit.

Following behind, Libby couldn't help noticing her aunt wasn't her usual tidy self. Her hair was escaping from her bun and her cardigan was fastened up the wrong way. It looked like she got ready in a hurry!

The station was completely deserted. Connie was scanning up and down, clearly trying to spot her dad. All around them were mountains covered in trees.

'I don't know where he's got to,' Connie sighed. She sat down on her case and searched for her phone in her rucksack.

Just then Miss Mousedale's phone rang. Libby wondered if it was Connie's mum calling to tell them they were delayed. But the look on her aunt's face suggested it wasn't someone she wanted to speak to. Her aunt's voice got louder. She was clearly upset about something. The only word Libby heard clearly was 'forgery'. Before she could find out more, she spotted a car in the distance.

'Is that your dad?' she shouted.

Connie's face lit up. She jumped to her feet and started waving. The car swung into the station and a tall boy jumped out. He had the same wild hair as Connie. It had to be Connie's brother, Libby thought.

'Fergus, what are you doing here? Where's Dad?'

'Well, that's a fine welcome,' Fergus laughed, scooping up Connie and spinning her around.

'Put me down,' Connie said. Her face was so red, her freckles had almost disappeared.

'Dad's too busy. I hear you've been really busy as well! Getting yourself into trouble, according to Mum.'

'I haven't seen him in months,' moaned Connie. 'This is my best friend Libby and her aunt, Miss Mousedale.'

'Hello,' said Fergus. 'So you must be the famous Libby. I've heard all about you and your mystery solving.'

Libby blushed. She really hoped Connie's family didn't really think she was a troublemaker.

Last term, Libby and Connie had discovered that their former teacher, Miss Browne, had framed her aunt for stealing a valuable brooch. They had uncovered her true identity, found the missing brooch and made sure she'd been captured by the *gendarmes* in Paris. But it was weeks ago, and only one mystery.

Miss Mousedale shivered and wrapped her cloak around herself tightly. 'We're looking forward to some peace and quiet. We've had enough excitement for one lifetime.'

'You'll be fine at our house, Miss Mousedale,' said Connie. '*Nothing* ever happens there.'

Libby silently groaned. She wasn't convinced that the countryside would be much fun, but with her mum still away in Peru she didn't have much choice. It had been really kind of Connie's family to invite her and her aunt to stay for the Christmas holidays. Maybe once they were back at the travelling school next term, there would be more adventures.

'It looks like it's going to rain.' Libby looked up. The clouds were gathering overhead and she was longing to get inside the car.

'More likely to be snow,' said Miss Mousedale. 'I remember those skies from my childhood and all those times we got snowed in at school.'

'Ooh, maybe we'll have a white Christmas!' said Libby.

'If you knew what it was like round here when it snowed, you wouldn't say that,' Connie laughed. 'Let's get inside. I'm freezing.'

Libby and Connie clambered into the backseat of an ancient, muddy Land Rover.

'I'm exhausted,' said Aunt Agatha. 'I barely slept a wink last night!'

Libby and Connie looked at each other and smirked. They knew for a fact that she had slept for most of the night.

'It won't be long now,' said Fergus after a few minutes. 'It's just down the track.'

Libby wiped the dirty window with her sleeve. She could see a long road lined with towering trees and in the distance she could just make out something large looming through the mist. *Surely that can't be Connie's house? It's huge,* thought Libby.

Four towers wrapped themselves around the house, sheltering it from the bitter wind. Behind was a forest of firs. As they approached the house, there was no sign of anyone or anything. Libby shivered as she looked up. Now she was nearer, she could see the crumbling brickwork and the patched up windows but it would be the biggest house she'd ever stayed in in her life.

'Home at last.' Connie rushed to the door, pushed it open and ran inside. 'Mum! Dad!' she shouted. 'Where are you?'

Libby was hit by a blast of heat from the open fire roaring away in the entrance hall. On either side of the fire were piles of logs and next to them were wellies in a mix of sizes and colours.

'Connie,' came a voice from the landing.

Libby looked up at the sweeping staircase ahead of them. The dark, red walls were filled with huge paintings. An older woman was coming down the stairs. She smiled but Libby noticed there were dark circles under her eyes.

'Mum!' Connie ran into her arms. 'Where's Dad?

I thought he was coming to pick us up?'

'He's in his study working, I'm afraid. We mustn't disturb him at the moment. He has some important business to attend to.'

Libby could see Connie was upset that her dad hadn't come out to say hello.

'It's so lovely to see you,' said Miss Mousedale, hugging Connie's mum. 'Thank you for having us both. Especially when things are so...'

Before she could finish her sentence, Connie's mum interrupted. 'You must all be starving. How about I get Mrs MacCallum to rustle you up some bacon and eggs?'

Libby wondered what her aunt had been about to say. What did she mean? But the thought of food quickly distracted her.

'Sounds perfect. We haven't eaten a thing in ages, Mrs Montgomery,' she said, winking at Connie.

Despite what they'd had on the train, the girls still managed to devour a whole plateful of cooked breakfast. Libby noticed that her aunt and Connie's mum were deep in conversation. She was trying to listen but Connie and Fergus were arguing about something.

'And do you know where she is now?' asked Connie's mum.

Aunt Agatha looked up. Libby turned away. She didn't want her aunt realising she'd been eavesdropping. Instead, she tried to join in with Connie and Fergus's conversation. 'What are you two arguing about?'

'This is us being nice,' laughed Connie. 'You should see when we're properly fighting.'

'Connie's a wild one,' said Fergus. 'Hadn't you noticed?'

'Am not,' said Connie, sticking her tongue out at him. And they started arguing again.

Libby looked over at her aunt and Connie's mum. Clearly their conversation had come to an end. She'd missed it.

'I think I'll have a rest. The journey took it out of me I'm afraid,' said her aunt.

'Come on Libby,' said Connie. 'Let's unpack. I'll show you where you're sleeping, Miss Mousedale.

Mum, have you put her in the blue guest room?' She headed up the stairs without waiting.

Connie's mum blushed, 'Agatha, I have put you in the room next to the girls. I hope that's okay? It seems a waste to open up the East Wing for one person. Not that I mean…' she stopped suddenly.

Libby watched Connie's mum fiddle with her necklace. Her face was turning blotchy. Libby really hoped she wasn't regretting inviting them to stay.

'It's fine, I understand,' said Miss Mousedale. 'Best that I'm near these two, you never know what mischief they'll get up to.'

Connie's mum smiled. 'Indeed. All that business with the police wasn't at all what I expected when I sent Connie to your school. Donal isn't convinced about her going to New York with you next term.'

'That would be a shame,' said Miss Mousedale. 'But I understand why it might not be appropriate, given the circumstances.'

Libby couldn't believe what she was hearing. *Surely Connie's mum didn't really mean she wouldn't be returning to school? What circumstances was her aunt talking about?* She couldn't imagine school without Connie.

'Libby, let's go and get changed. Then I can show you around,' shouted Connie. Libby could see she was eager to get away. Bertie and James galloped down the corridor and ran up towards her. They were barking excitedly around Connie's feet.

'Connie, how many times have I told you about encouraging them to go upstairs. They'll get mud everywhere.'

'Sorry, Mum. I promise I won't let them stay long, I've just missed them.' Connie dashed upstairs. Libby hurried behind her.

Libby stopped as she reached the top of the stairs. She took a closer look at the large paintings. It was like being in a museum. There was even a suit of armour stood menacingly in the corner. Her home was tiny in comparison. You could have fitted all of their things into just the landing.

'Weird, to think all the people in those portraits lived here,' said Connie. 'But don't worry it's definitely not a haunted house!'

Libby hesitated as Connie disappeared down the dark corridor. Despite Connie's reassurances, she couldn't help but imagine their ghosts lingering around watching her. If she was going to stay here, she mustn't let her imagination get carried away.

She was just about to move again, when she felt a hand on her shoulder and froze.